I0524278

Angel's Share

By

Seymour Hamilton

Illustrated by Shirley Mackenzie

Copyright 2021 by Seymour Hamilton

All rights reserved. The use of any part of this publication reproduced, transmitted in any form or by any means, electronic, mechanical, photocopying recording, or otherwise, or stored in a retrieval system, without the prior written consent of the publisher, or in the case of photocopying or other reprographic copying, a licence from the Canadian Copyright Licensing Agency—is an infringement of the copyright law.

Library and Archives Canada Catalogue

Hamilton, Seymour

Angel's Share

Published by Seymour Hamilton "Colophon"

ISBN: 9780994949981

This is a work of fiction. Names, characters, and incidents are the products of the author's imagination. Any resemblance to actual events, or persons, living or dead, in the past or present, is entirely coincidental.

Cover art and page illustrations by Shirley MacKenzie, whose portfolio can be viewed at www.shirleymackenzie.com

Formatting the cover and the layout by Mary Montague.

Visit the author at www.SeymourHamilton.com or on Facebook at www. facebook.com/seymour.hamilton.5

Contents

Angel's Share

by

Seymour Hamilton

A Story from the World of

The Astreya Trilogy

about how Able Angel

helped establish Matris

as told to Astreya and Lindey

when they returned from the Village.

Angel's Share

It can't be called "whisky" until the
distillate or "spirit" has been aged
for years in oak casks.
During this long maturing process,
the distinctive flavours ripen.
Some of the spirit is absorbed
into the casks.
This loss is called "ullage."
Some of the maturing whisky evaporates.
Distillers call this, "The Angels' Share".

Acknowledgements

The Old Salt Press

Special thanks to Shirley MacKenzie for the cover and illustrations that helped me visualize and understand what became our characters.

Rick Spilman saw an early version and made insightful comments that led to important revision and re-writing.

Joan Druett gave invaluable advice that immensely improved the story, and did so with the understanding and professionalism of the excellent writer of history and fiction that she is.

Mary Montague greatly improved the formatting of the paperback version by reorganizing the endpapers, completing the cover layout and giving Shirley Mackenzie's illustrations the clarity they deserve.

As with those stories that went before, this book would not have been written were it not for the patience, understanding, and encouragement of my wife, Katherine Fletcher.

One

I always knew I was going to be all right, no matter what.

It ain't reasonable, I know, considering that the entire bloodstained universe ain't fair, but that's what I believed. And still do. Now, before you get to thinking that I'm one of them credulous bastards what believes sunny days are just over the horizon, I got to add that me being all right is one of a very small bunch of beliefs that I have any time for.

I'm getting ahead of meself. Telling you what I think about life is supposed to come later, once I've gotten into me story. When you're hooked, I'll can give you the benefit of all the wisdom what I've been stowing in me hold all these years.

So, back to the beginning.

I'm not much different from most folks: one ma, one da, no sibs. Ma didn't live too long. Fact is, I never knew her to remember much, so Da was me leading hand, so to speak. Except he weren't there most of the time, and when he was, I couldn't wait for him to leave. A hard voice me Da had, and a harder fist, what he often used on anyone he could best, and a fair slice of time on me -- when he could catch me. The women what he called me step-moms he larmered hard and regular, but they could run off, as they all of them eventually did, and nobody to say them anything but congratulations for getting out from under the thumb of a rare nasty bastard.

Until I was more or less grown up and looking after meself, there was always one of them unlucky women -- quite a few of them over the years too, 'cause women thought Da had the face of an angel -- and me too -- at least, that's what one of them told me. She went on to talk about other parts of him, too, but I'll spare you the blushes what comes of hearing what's best left unsaid. Anyway, there's nothing like living a lie, so Da called himself Angel from then on, and since he was me pa, I got the name, too, like, "Yer Angel's brat, ain'tcha?" That's when I wasn't being called "Hey you!" and "Wharf rat, look lively or I'll give you such a bloody smack."

Round about the time that most boys are getting their small sliver of education from the local whoever what dishes it out for cash, I was still innocent and ignorant. Well, ignorant, anyway, 'cause paid education ain't in the cards for a sailor's son living' down in dockland where nobody goes 'lest he has to, and nobody stays innocent long when there's plenty of work that's done mostly at night with no questions asked or answered. I was lucky. I found me an old codger what was willing to teach me to read, write a bit and get beyond counting on me fingers and toes, which was usually bare and right some cold for half the year. Back then, I thought I found him, but I know now that it was him what did the finding. He seemed ancient to me at the time, but now's I think about it, I'd be calling him a young feller if he showed up on me doorstep this morning the way you two did.

His name was Al. Not Alan or Albert, nor Alphonse, Aloysius nor Alouitious neither. If he ever had more than the two letters to his name, he never told me, nor anyone else. He were a seaman, you could tell. Short one finger on his left hand where he decided that losing a knuckle were better than a quick trip below with the anchor, what he'd got himself tangled up in by reason of being a bit slow when it was let go from the cat-head. He told me that one himself, when he was enjoying the pint he always drank at the end of our lessons in book learning. He finished the tale by saying, "Let that keep you respectful of the fact that it ain't all in books, lad."

He had more'n a few of such sailor's yarns. He was a sea-daddy to me, even though we was on land the whole time. He made me honour me ma what had left me, and me step-ma's as well. He protected me from me Da more'n once, too, specially when me progenitor — how'd you like that word he taught me? — was after drink taken. It was Al what made me un-scared of Da, because I saw he weren't scared of him, and that showed me I didn't have to be, either.

When I think back, I can still hear him getting me started our first day with the numbers. "Now follow me, lad," he said and began the old sing-song: pom, pom ti pom. Two ones are two, two two's are four, two threes are six…and so on up to twelve twelves, which came a good many days and weeks later.

He taught me reading as well. Where he got the books, I'll never know, but most of them was some old and real musty, like they'd been too long in a cellar and were only a damp day away from being a rat's mattress. There were books with numbers, what had their white spaces around the edges all scribbled up by whoever had owned them first -- and maybe second and third.

An 'there was the book that Al made me wash me hands before I touched 'cause he said it was what Holy writ. He never exactly told me who Holy was, 'cause he had a notion that if you named him, her or it, you'd be followed by no end of bad luck to the end of your days, which you'd be wanting to come right speedily, it would be that horrible. Al said it was all right to say the name of the blokes who had done the actual writing down, because they was Holy's amanuensis. There's another pricy word he told me. Al told me Holy had many of them amanuensises, each of them a righteous sort, what had little patience with the rest of the world. They were mostly "Woe unto ye…" folks, although there was one what Al called Singing Solly who wrote a whole lot about his wife. Al told me it was all about love, and that I should put it out of me head until I was much older, and since I was of an age when boys steer clear of girls anyway, I did just that. Back then, I didn't have the experience to tell if it were true or one of those songs the lads sing when their mothers ain't listening.

Al liked me to read him stuff he already knew by heart, so he could correct me. First time he did it, I near dropped the book. I was gobsmacked that he would know not just the next word or two, like you do when someone gets you going on a song you've sung before, but could go on and on, page after page, with me reading along like we was doing a chorus together.

He sure liked the writings of those old folks with names like Hosea, who was all about destruction; Nehemiah, who was a bit more cheerful but not by much; Job, who Holy never gave an even break; Jonah, the unlucky one who every sailor fears to meet, and jawbreaking Habakuk, the sad sack, who was a rare old whiner to Holy about them who he thought deserved to be smited or smote or however you say the word for getting whacked. Thanks to all of them, I heard more than I care to remember about smiting and getting smoted by Holy, who for sure wasn't what you might call friendly. But what can you do with or for a god who says from the outset that he's some powerful and serious jealous? Try not to cross him, I guess. But there were so many ways how you could bring down Holy's wrath, from messing with his name to coveting your neighbour's house, wife, ass, ox, manservant, maidservant or whatever. I wasn't interested in anyone's ox, ass, or manservant. What's more, I didn't know no maidservants, so I decided to keep it that way for safety's sake.

Many a time, Al would end up our reading sessions with Holy's Ecclesiastes, a preacher-man who was long on advice. "Remember now thy Creator in the days of thy youth, when the evil days come not nor the years draw nigh when thou shalt say, 'I have no pleasure in them.'" That were one of Al's favourite bits. On and on he'd go together with me reading right to the end of them little numbered bits until we both fetched up with the last words "… of making many books there is no end, and much study is a weariness of the flesh." Then he'd mutter his favourite saying: "It ain't all in books, lad."

That was when he'd wink at me -- a kind'a twitch of one blue eye under a great awning of an eyebrow -- and call for a pint. "So tell me another," I'd ask, and he'd spin a yarn for me, perhaps from some book he'd lost along the way, perhaps something what had happened to him.

One time, he looked into the middle distance and spoke low and soft. "I believe my love more fair than any she belied with false compare." "Go on," I said. "Tell me about her," but by that time he had his nose in his pint, and wouldn't say no more -- till another day, when perhaps he'd give me the words that came first, but only if I could remember what he'd said before. It made me listen, I can tell you, and learn right quick. Made it fun for me, like a competition 'tween him and me, even when what he was teaching me wasn't stories or songs.

Part of what he taught me was that there are different kinds of words: the grubby work-day words that I'd learned growing up by the wharves, and the book-learned words that hang together in an orderly fashion what makes sense. Al showed me there's more: words with power, the ones what sing to themselves and make you glad that they're coming out of your mouth. He made me swap between the ways of talking, so that one day I'd be sounding all of a piece like we was loading barges and slanging the sonumbitch in charge, and the next, speaking distinctly and with great precision as if I actually was the muck-a-muck who gives the orders.

Always we'd come back to what he called poetry. Stuff like, "For thy sweet love remembered such wealth brings that then I scorn to change my state with kings." But he'd never tell me who she was what he had loved so much that when he said the words the corners of his eyes filled up, so's he had to knuckle them dry and sniff.

After five or more years, when Al had me to the place where I was looking for more to read, learn, and figure out on me own, one morning he weren't there anymore. The publican at the inn where Al lived told me he'd gone away with money owing on the slate, so I paid up for him from what I earned running errands, crewing the harbour ferry, fetching stuff, cutting bait, rowing seamen to their girls, and girls to where the seamen's ships was anchored -- all the ways a bright lad can make a handful of coins until his Da shows up and took it away like it was his right and privilege, along with a thump across me ear, like as not. I never cried from that, but I cried for Al. After a couple days when he weren't where he should a 'been, they fished him out of the harbour, all nibbled by fishes so's I could only tell it was him by his hand.

Da found me when I'd got back from showing the harbour master where Al's finger wasn't, so's he'd be buried proper with a name over him even if it was only two letters. I was blubbering quietly to meself in the room in the chandler's shed Da called his, what I paid for so I had somewhere to be when he was off at sea doing stuff he didn't tell nobody. He had sneaked in dead quiet, and had been standing there until I heard his foot move and I looked up, me nose all snotty and me eyes raw from rubbing them. Instead of his usual paternal greeting of a quick slap up the back of me head, he laughed at me. Without thinking, I jumped to me feet and hit him on the nose hard enough so's I heard it crack. And then when he was doubled up, eyes and nose running into his hands, 'cause that's what you do when you get hit a good shot on the beak, I was around him and out the door before he could get himself together. I'd seen him fight more'n once, and he was good -- meaning real nasty. Head-butting, eye-gouging and biting if he was losing, and doing kick-face and knee-crotch if he got the better of someone.

So I kept going till I was dockside, looking behind for me avenging parent, feeling desperate, when a sailor caught me by the shoulder, pointed me at an empty dory that someone had just tied up and left there, dropped his kitbag into the stern and told me to get weaving. Off we went, me rowing, him looking at me like he was wondering about what had made me lose me professional calm with which I usually plied me trade as a seasoned wharf-rat. Over his shoulder, I seen Da on the dock, waving his fist and shouting words nobody should yell at any man, least of all his son. The wind was from where we were going, but the sailor heard them right enough to guess that I was adrift.

"Need a berth, all found, no questions asked?" he asked. I didn't even think about it. I nodded and kept pulling on me oars. "Then swing a bit to starboard into the lee of that big schooner what's getting ready for sea." I nodded again, this time beginning to ask meself what I was getting into.

"Five years," he said, like he'd heard me brains at work. "Are you willing and able?" "Yes to both," I said. Just then the wind blew me a few more words from Da that are not fit for writing down, so I nodded again.

"I'm Smitty to me friends," he says to me. "Leading Hand Smith to the officers on the quarterdeck. What do they call you?"

"Angel's son," I started to say, but it just came out "Angel."

"You said you were willing and able, so Able Angel you'll be."

And that's how I got me name and ran away to sea..

Two

So, young feller, you want to hear some more? You too, lass?

Well, I won't tell ye about learning the ropes from Smitty, 'cause you know all about that; and you also know what can't be told 'cause it's made of wind and water and being afraid and carrying on anyway, and laughing your fool head off afterwards with them who was there with you when bad things almost happened but didn't. Smitty kept me from lots of ways I could'a come to grief at sea and ashore. Bailed me out of trouble with drink and what passes for the law in more than a couple of our ports of call, and thank you very much now, Smitty, 'cause I didn't say so back then.

I can tell you that the five years went by slow as the graveyard watch and fast as that first drink slides down when you're in good company. In the beginning, it were endless, stretching out in front of me longer than a lifetime. And as it went on, what was behind me kind'a folded up on itself like the middle of a musical squeeze-box, and what was still up ahead was like the horizon on a clear day: bright and close and beckoning with the promise that there'll soon be something interesting shoving its head up over that long line where the sky and sea meet and kiss.

Somewhere about year two or three, all of us knew that everything was getting different, and not in a good way. Storms in winter is one thing, but it don't seem fair when you get them when old sailors is telling you there'll be summer sailing. And everyone knows it ain't going well at all at all when somehow, without a word said by anyone, y'can see that the master's worried.

When we made port to do the trading that's the masters 'and owners 'reasons for building, crewing and working their ships, we'd hear ugly stories about a southern sickness moving north, and of crops failing and folk dying mysterious-like, and fights breaking out at the edges between town and country because money wouldn't buy what little food there was, and those that had what was needful had figgered out that all the money they was being offered wasn't something they could eat. It got so folks was taking without paying -- and taking lives, too. 'Course, there was some what banded together, helping each other out, but that didn't always work when there was others desperate enough to pillage, loot and kill. Lucky for us, we stayed abreast'a most of the ugliness that we heard about more and more about as time went on. Howsomever, I was young, and dying was something that happened to old people — older than what I was, anyway.

I didn't take death serious until the night I was standing watch with Smitty in a nasty bit of a blow. We was tearing along on the starboard tack under double-reefed main, bare pole on the mizzen and only the storm jib ahead of the foremast; punching our bowsprit into every second wave. We was standing in shin deep in water spilling down the length of the ship -- and we was amidships on the high side. He'd just told me to hang onto the safety lines if I had to cross the deck, like I wasn't white-knuckling the rope as he spoke, when for some reason I never figgered out, he let go, and a wave took him. Just like that. One moment he was there, then there was a wave, and there he wasn't. All the screaming and hollering and swearing I could do wouldn't change nothin'. No turning back in that weather, either. A piece torn right out of the ship, the crew -- and me.

I'd known folk what had died. Me Ma, before I could remember anything except a great big hole where she wasn't. An' Al, too, but when I lost him, I never saw it happen. Losing Smitty was different. I was older, see, and it happened sudden, while I was watching. Shook me up, I can tell you, cause Smitty had taught me so well I didn't even know how much I'd been changed. From smooth-chinned, smart-arse wharf-rat to confident, shaving-daily, able seaman in only four going on five years.

But I was telling you about the way things were going overall — the march of history, as Al would say — and I got off course and into me own heavy weather.

Well, whatever was happening in that universal grand parade into the uncertain future, Nair, our master, had no problem with making smart deals with scared people, so we had full holds every leg of our way north, and a heavy strongbox in the stern cabin, too, I'll wager. The master was canny, which is only a couple of points to loo'ard of greedy, but he took care of his ship, and us too, not that we were all that pleased when he anchored when he could have docked, and took only a couple of steady hands with him when he went ashore to bargain, buy and sell. We missed our shore leave, but we knew the ship came first. Nair sure did: he laid in spare spars, cordage, metalwork and the kind of provisions that last a lot longer than they're what yer call appealing, much less tasty. And because he took us further and further north, he kitted us out with good gear that held most weather out; and though we grumbled, we took what we were given and used it well.

While we were getting used to visiting ports of call what were mostly smaller than the piss-pot town where I was born, I was beginning me fifth year aboard and wondering if I'd sign on again, 'cause I could see the trading getting harder and the rumours uglier. Afloat were dangerous, no question about that, but though me shipmates bickered and skirmished around, in the end, we hung together for the sake of the ship. It ain't that way ashore, where it's every man for hisself. O 'course, spite of me asking myself about what and how I'd choose, in the end there weren't no choice at all.

Stella -- did I tell you the name of me ship? -- needed her bottom scraped and her rigging renewed and a couple of sprung yards replaced with those new spars we'd been collecting. So the master took us into a high-sided bay with a fair-sized river at its head. After we'd anchored in the stream for a day or so to wash some of the sea growth off the ship's bottom, we dropped back to where the tide dried us out on a hard gravel bank. Then all hands and the cook worked for three hours at low water, and then lay around at anchor while the tide turned, and then did it all over again on the other side of the ship. Loads of soggy, wet, bottom-scraping fun, but good-tasting fresh water from the river and no watches to stand.

On day three of all this diverting entertainment, we was not alone. Two more ships joined us, one after the other, coming around the headland like great white swans furling their wings as they settle onto the water. Living aboard *Stella* when she was wearing the sails I helped set, I never saw her from a distance; so when the other ships hove into view, I was some impressed. One of the old hands told me that their proper names were *Tidewalker* and *Silver Swan*, but to us the hands, they were *Wetfoot* and the *Dirty Duck*. *Wetfoot* was first alongside us, and a neat job she made of it, too. I'd not seen staysail rig before, and I marvelled at how few men it took to handle her canvass. Then the *Dirty Duck* came into view, with her crossed-yard topsail still set on her foremast to catch the evening wind what was bringing her between the headlands and into the bay. As she ghosted up, wind over tide and current, she, too came alongside us so neat you'd think we didn't need the fenders we'd hung out against her arrival.

I was on the detail what was positioning a gangway between the ships when I looked up at the sailor doing the other half of the job aboard the Duck and saw a girl's face looking at me. She wore faded-out brown breeks and shirt, the same what we all wore aboard *Stella*, but there was more inside her shirt than there was under mine, if you takes me meaning.

One of me mates had to give me a shove to get me back to working, 'cause I was staring at her, flummoxed, with me gob half open, so's I near to dropped me end. After I belayed the lines holding the gangway in place, I looked about and saw that most of the crew of the *Dirty Duck* was women, and that included the leading hands and officers. Soon as I got me head around that, I saw the kids. Now you got to understand that nobody takes women and children aboard — at least, that was all I knew til then. What really took me aback was that the littlies — the crawlers, the toddlers and the staggerers — was all on the quarterdeck between safety-nets, with two nursemaids in charge of keeping them out of mischief. As you well know, the quarterdeck is officer country, where the crew don't go unless they have orders to be there, which was why I was gobsmacked to see the kiddies messed up underfoot of the master and the mates.

While I was standing about, mouth open, taking all of this in, the *Duck's* master crossed over the gangway I'd just finished putting in position. She was a woman, and a tall, black-haired, good looking one at that, and not that much older than me so's I could appreciate her.

Right after that, I heard a couple old hands snorting with laughter at the way I was gawping. They'd known what was coming, of course, but would they tell me there was women aboard the ships they'd named? Not a chance. It was their idea of a joke on the young feller I was at the time, 'cause I was so sure I knew it all after only four years at sea.

Nair greeted the other masters like they was family, which weren't all that surprising considering that the three of them were tall, slim, black-haired, green-eyed over high cheek-bones, and very much in command of theirselves and their crews. A couple of words from any one of them, and things got done right quick and no mistake. Hard to say why. It were one of them things that just happens when a master is in command. You know it at once, just like it don't take no time at all to know when it ain't there, when the skipper is making do with bluster and shouting.

Anyhoo, they stood talking and eyeballing each other's ships and each other like they was pleased with what they saw, and then all of them went down to the master's cabin.

I got to talking with some of the old hands what had laughed at me, and they told me that the woman was Meissa, master of *Silver Swan* and daughter to Zubin the Grand Master. She, and our master Nair and the other master, Markab, was close like family. It was hard to tell how old they were, 'cause everybody calls his master 'the old man' even when it's you what's older, and because there's something about giving orders that makes a man seem older -- and a woman too, I guess. Thinking about it now, I can tell you that they was all real young to be masters: but back then, I paid it no mind.

A bit later, the three crews was enjoying the pleasure of visiting aboard each other's ships and messing together all at once on account of not having no sea duties -- except for the cooks and the unlucky sod standing anchor watch 'cause he pulled the short straw. Some of our crew were paying a call on the other ships, and some of the other crews were visiting *Stella*. I was sitting between two of me mates, the ones who'd laughed at me earlier, so I began quizzing them. It had never occurred to me that *Stella* had sister-ships, so I needed educating, which they was happy to do, reminding me all the while that I was an ignorant young sprout what didn't know nothin'.

I found out there was twelve ships, led by Grand Master Zubin aboard the biggest of the schooners, *Cygnus*, what the hands called *Chicken*. Then they rhymed off the other ships 'names, both what was carved on the name-boards on their hulls and what the hands called them, along with the names of their masters. And that were a whole other story, because most of the masters had been given new names by Zubin -- like our master, who he re-named Nair when he gave him command of *Stella*.

When they got to talking about the masters, it got right some confusing. Sometimes they were using the masters' shore-going names, then a moment later, the names they had from Zubin, and then the ships 'names, too -- like the master and the ship were one and the same. I lost interest about then, because over their shoulders I could see the girl whose deep brown eyes I'd looked into as we were fixing up the gangway, and she were looking at me, and after a bit, the two of us were eyeballing each other, just starin', and by then I weren't hearing nothin'.

All around the mess deck, the hands was drinking a second or a third pint, what was the tradition after scraping and painting, and I was getting to me feet and about to stroll, casual-like, over to where those eyes was beckoning me like two bright harbour lights on a dark night, when Master Nair's steward taps me on the shoulder and tells me I'm wanted aft. First off, I thought he was joking, put up to it by me mates to stop me eyes and them brown eyes from getting any closer. Then he turns me around with his two hands in me hair, and gives me a little slap on the cheek, just a friendly pat, and mutters something about being sorry to take me away from me hopes and inclinations -- though he used some of them other words with which I won't burden your tender shell-like ears, lass.

As we made our way astern, I started running through in me mind what I'd been up to in the past few days. I hadn't hardly been in the stern cabin since signing on, more'n four years gone, 'cause I'd been keeping me nose clean and me ears and eyes open. All the way down the stern companionway I couldn't think of nothing that would bring down the skipper's wrath on me head, but when you're young, you can never be sure. I thought about how it must have been, back when old Habakkuk was saying "Woe unto ye sinners," and wondered if I was about to get some woe meself.

After living in close quarters for'ard along with the rest of the crew, the first thing I thought when the door opened in front of me was how much room there was in the stern cabin, and all of it for only one man. You'd almost forget you was aboard till you saw the familiar curve of the ship's side. Lots of light, too, pouring in from the big, glassed-in scuttles on the ship's stern. Even with the three skippers sitting around a table, there was space all around them. You'd almost forget you was aboard 'til you saw the familiar curve of the ship's side. At first, I couldn't see any of them clearly with the light behind them, but they could see me. I could feel it, too, like they was peeling back the skin on me head to find out what was inside.

"Able seaman Angel," said Nair. "Tell us how you got your name."

I don't remember what I said, but I spoke the best way Al taught me, so it must have come out all right, 'cause I could sort of see their faces soften a bit, like they were interested in me and me story, and maybe surprised I could talk without mumbling and grunting and cursing and the like. Anyway, when I was finished, Nair nodded.

"He's known as Able," he said to his fellow skippers, "and it's a name he's earned. I don't have to tell you that most nicknames aren't nearly as complimentary."

Embarrassing it was, but a whole lot better than being the object of what old Habakkuk would have called "the smiting." I stood a bit easier, wondering what was coming next.

"Able, Master Markab has a need for a man who knows his way around your home port. We know it's been more than four years since you were there, but your knowledge of the lay of the land is the best we've got. The plan is for *Tidewalker* to transport a couple dozen people to … to a place where they want to live. Unfortunately, it's not just a simple matter of picking them up off the dock at high tide. In the time since you lived ashore, the people in just about all the ports we visit have become … ah … less friendly with strangers, particularly people from the south, like those that *Wet* … ah … *Tidewalker* plans to take as passengers. The people in the ports and harbours trade with us because they need what we've got, but they have no time for people from up country, which is what they call farmers and the folk what live further ashore, and in particular, further south, where things are going to hell in a hand-basket. I can tell you that up country is in bad shape, Able. You may have heard of hunger, lawlessness and the like, and it's all true and worse than you can imagine."

I nodded. There was scuttlebutt talk that things ashore were going serious bad, but I hadn't heard it like fact, 'stead of a shipboard rumour, what I'd long since learned not to trust.

"Master Markab needs you to meet the … the passengers … and shepherd them to where they can be ferried to *Tidewalker* without their being seen and … apprehended."

I didn't much like the pause before the last long word, which I knew was one of those what important people like to use for times when you or me would use sharp, ugly little words — like "whacked," for instance. Master Nair must have guessed what I was thinking, because he set the hook real quick.

"Get it right, Able, and you'll be in line for advancement. Get it wrong, and you'll share the fate of the … passengers … when the townies find out who they are … and where they're from."

Again, there was that very loud silence between some of the words what made me worry a bit, but not enough to stop the word "advancement" from making me dead keen. Meet some lubbers, form them up, lead them to the boats, get them aboard the ship — piece of cake, I thought. I'll be a leading hand before me twenty-first birthday.

So I said, "At your command, Master."

I must have looked some eager, because all three of them kind of settled back in their chairs, like the job was done.

"So then, get your kit aboard *Tidewalker*, and await further instructions from Master Markab."

Off I went, wondering what I'd got meself into. By the time I had mustered me kit, the girl with the eyes had gone back aboard the *Dirty Duck*. I never got to tell her that I had been transferred to *Wetfoot*.

Three

Changing ships is always rough at first. Yer don't know nobody, nobody knows you. Yer might think that was also true about when I first joined *Stella*, but then I was brand new, absolute beginner, bottom of the pecking order, and though that meant I was in for some teasing, it were pretty much all of it good natured. Coming fresh into a crew what's known each other for years, you're suspect. Anything you do that's strange to them, you get questions like, "Is that what you did on your last ship? Must be a bunch of lubbers, then. Or was it just you, and that's why they got rid of you?" You can't answer that kind of thing, and trying only makes it worse.

You know that no two ships do everything exactly the same way, even if they're both three-masted schooners. Aboard *Wetfoot*, I had to learn the ropes for handling staysails on the two forward masts, 'stead of the gaff-and-boom system I knew so well aboard *Stella*. They're all sails to be raised, set, trimmed and struck, except staysails are easier to raise and strike, but when me new shipmates saw me looking for throat and peak halyards, they had a good laugh.

Now then, you have to know that when it comes to shortening sail, your basic gaff-and-boom rigged schooner has reef points above the foot of the sails, what you use to gather the canvass around the boom, reducing yer sail area. Well, when a staysail's too big for the weather, what yer do is take it down and put up a smaller one. Or none. Or strike one on the foremast and set one on the mizzen. It has to do with the balancing of the forces. But it's not quite like yer regular schooner where you can feel the wind right in the slot a'tween jibs, stays'ls, fores'ls. mizzen, and mainsails and sense the breeze sliding across the canvass and sucking the whole ship forward -- and you over the side, too, if you don't hold on. On a staysail schooner there are more slots, I guess you might say, and getting all of them working together is quite the trick.

I see you nodding yer head like you know it all, and the lass going all glassy eyed again, so I'll spare you the rest of me brilliant observations on the relative merits of gaff and staysail rigs, not to mention the niceties of sail-handling on the different kinds of schooner.

Suffice it to say — in the words of them writers of the old books what Al had me read — suffice it to say, we made an easy passage south, with me shaking down among me new messmates without no serious breeches of nautical discipline, if you don't count me showing a trick of the wrist and elbow to the blowhard on me watch, what action on me part was generally taken as being a good thing by all who saw, and most of those who heard. You got to choose real careful who you stroke, and who you thump, and that time, I got it right.

You might think that as *Wetfoot* eased into me home port that late spring Sunday morning that I'd be all choked up with the thought of returning to me birthplace, but all I could think of was how I'd left, and how little I wanted to see me Da. Y'see, in some ways, I was still the boy who'd popped him on the nose and then run away to sea. I couldn't get it into me head that I was now closing in on five years older, best part of a handspan taller, a whole lot bigger and healthier and tougher than the snot-nosed kid who'd figgered that the best thing to do was run away — a long way away.

So I stood a'tween the foremast staysail and the jib, where the leading hand couldn't see me, and looked out at the wharves, and behind them at the sheds and the shops and the inns and pubs, an further back at the houses, and up the hill to the mansions where the ship-owners lived, and on up to the spire on the church that rose above the skyline to give us mariners a leading mark for finding our way into the harbour. And it all came back to me, like I was looking at a picture what I'd drawn meself, because I knew what was behind the houses, overhung by the roofs and shaded by the occasional tree, because I'd walked and run all them roads and lanes and alleys, starting from the first time I wandered away from one of me step-moms and got proper lost, dirty and hungry, before she found me, smacked me bum and carted me back home.

Then as I was staring, I startled as a hand fell on me shoulder, and Master Markab was standing beside me. I flinched a second time when he spoke real loud, so's he could be overheard by the crew.

"Right, Angel, You're my man ashore. Find the passengers, see that they've got their fee for passage, lead them to the boats, get them aboard. You're coming with me to make the final arrangements. I'm going below now, and when I'm back on deck, I want you waiting in the starboard longboat together with …."

And then he called out three of the older hands. I guessed he was making sure there wouldn't be anyone wandering off in search of drink and women. Now it's all history, I can tell you that he was also making sure that I'd be the one to blame if it all went sideways and he had to clear his ship of anything that had gone down wrong ashore.

Not much later, when *Stella*'s sails was struck, but not harbour-furled, and she was hanging on one anchor set into the river bottom so's she was rode by the current, whatever the tide, Markab had one of the longboats launched and we was pulling towards the wharves. When Markab and me was on the dock, he had the men in the boat wait, making it right clear that anyone not there when he got back, best be able to swim.

"Listen, lad, there's got to be a slop shop close. Take me there."

So I did as he said, and in no time we was under a sign reading "Samuel's Nautical Tailoring," what everyone called "Sammy's Slops." Sunday or no, in we went, and to me massive surprise, Master Markab kitted me out like an officer: a fair pair of boots, black britches, white shirt and a blue jacket, all of them nearly new, plus a mate's peaked hat, just like the brass-trimmed one he was wearing, only plain.

"You'll do," he said when I'd shifted into them. "Have his old kit taken to my longboat, Mr. Samuel. Now we're going to church. Look like you're used to it."

Feeling that for sure I'd be rumbled by the quality what was walking in pairs and families up the hill to the church, I put meself a pace astern, and half a pace to port of the Master, and did whatever he did while keeping me mouth shut. I'd never been inside a church before, so it were all new to me, and at first, fascinating. When we was sat down waiting for the show to start, I got to looking around, cautious-like, so's nobody would think I was gawping. Right away, I started to recognize some of the faces of the older men now they'd got their Sunday hats off, among them a couple ship owners I knew from when I was still a nipper. In church, they was all busy looking important, not at all like when they were shouting at the wharfies. An 'I also saw more'n a couple respectable merchants who'd had me running errands from the wharves to their businesses, what were near enough to the wharfs to make delivery quick, and far enough to keep the rough folk away, all nicely worked out so that the quality felt comfortable in their stores. Sitting there in a pew beside Markab, for a little while I was afraid one of them would tumble to who I was, but what with me in me nice new rig, and with the changes in me size and bearing what came from the years at sea, their eyes just slid right over me.

Well, there was praying and singing and listening to a reading what the parson thought was important enough for him to preach us a great long and some boring sermon about brotherly love and understanding and getting right by his Lord, who wasn't much like old Al's Holy. The preacher's Lord wasn't into smiting. According to him, Lord was all about forgiveness and looking after orphans and the fatherless, and even the stranger within thy gates. He ran on like poetry to say that they all shall eat and be satisfied, so that the Lord thy God may bless thee in all the work of thine hand which thou doest.

I began to wonder if maybe I was due for some serious eating and drinking meself, that is until Master Markab bent his head towards me ear and whispered, "No chance of so much as a free drink from this lot." I kept me face straight, but it shook me a bit, 'cause 'til then, I had been thinking that maybe Markab was serious-minded about his church-going.

Well, after a few more prayers and another hymn, we was out the door, shaking the preacher's hand and mingling with the faithful — or at least with the folks who'd been in the church, what ain't necessarily the same, I can tell you right easy. Master Markab had his hand shook by the skippers and the merchants, and a couple times held for a moment by the gloved fingers of their wives, and he murmured about how nice it was to be here together after so long at sea. I was almost beginning to enjoy meself and look into the eyes of the young women what were standing beside their Ma's and Da's, when a pious-looking feller all in black singled out Master Markab and pulled him aside. He did one of those grab-the-other-feller's-hand-and-cover-both-with-yer-spare-hand handshakes that men do when they want you to believe they're honest. If either of them said anything, I didn't hear. Then the Master touched me on the shoulder and we headed off towards the sea.

We walked back down the hill with the church spire a bright spear behind us, all lit up by the sun. Down we went into the shadows where the afternoon sun wasn't, where Markab slowed to take a quick look at a piece of paper that hadn't been in his hand before the handshake.

"Foaming wold," he mutters as he slides the paper into his pocket." Here's a pair of ducks: I can read this, but I don't know the town. The lad knows the town, but he can't read."

"Begging yer pardon," I says, "I can read," what was true, "and I'm not a lad anymore," what was cheeky.

He hesitated for a heartbeat, took me arm and led me into a pub we was passing, and he sat me down at a small table under a smokey old lantern. We were almost the only customers there, it being Sunday when all good men and true was spozed to be with their wives and families. When we each had a mug in one hand, he produced the piece of paper and we looked at it together.

"Meet about twenty travellers before dawn where the road crosses the stream and then head south along the stream to the wharves. Say the name of your ship."

"Mean anything to you?" the Master asks me, keeping his voice low.

"That's what we call the marsh road. Been up there by the stream many a time," I tell him. "It's soft and wet. I used to go looking for fiddleheads in the spring, and little brown trout you can scoop up in yer hand, if yer quick. It ain't much more than a summer short-cut, and at this time of year it's only beginning to dry out, but it'll do to

get them down to the south side of town where the boats can pick
them up."

I slopped a little beer onto the table and drew him a rough map,
showing where the road going north runs beside a stream for a bit,
and then crosses it close to where the marsh road begins, and then
curves around the hill with the church on it, where it splits to double
back towards the north end of town, or goes on nor'eastward, to cross
the river.

"I'll go up the marsh road, meet the passengers by the bridge
and lead them back down to where you'll have the boats waiting. But
we'll all have to be right smart and some early, or the town's going
to be up and wondering what's happening when there's ships' boats
where none of them ever goes."

At that moment, in comes a passel of men, all of them excited
and looking for drink. It weren't that we was overhearing them : they
was talking l just a bit less than a shout, and they was all doing it at
the same time.

"… gonna be a fight …"

"… up country folks ready to attack..."

"… caught one of 'em…"

"… plan on coming down the swamp road…"

"… and after that, he started talking for fair…"

"… they'll be waiting in the woods for first light…"

"… looking to raid the shops and warehouses…"

"… hoping to surprise us, but we're ready for 'em…"

"… we'll stop 'em...."

"…send 'em back where they came from."

"… but only a few. Enough to warn the others that we're
serious."

What they was saying got more confused after that, as they
called for beer or whiskey, and sat themselves down around the
tables. Some of them took knives and short clubs out of their belts or

pockets and laid them beside their drinks, trying to show they was hard men.

Markab shoved his beer mug back and forth, rubbing out the map I'd made. We looked at each other.

"Well, that tears it to shreds. We're here for a couple dozen people, including women and children, with all their baggage together with a … a cargo … which is my fee. They'll all be coming along a muddy path, expecting to arrive at dawn and get loaded into boats. And they're going to walk straight into a bunch of drunk, angry, scared, stupid lubbers, all of 'em looking for a fight."

"Maybe the feller they caught was unlucky, but he was smart," I said. "The townies don't know about the women and children. They're expecting a raiding party."

"Makes no difference. It was never a good plan, but now it's scuppered. We'd better go back to the ship. If I stay around to collect my fee I'll lose it to the townies for sure."

When Markab said that, I knew he was in it for the money, and nothing else. He was all set to leave men, women and families not just stranded, but beat up as well. But I knew what would keep him in the game.

"Master, when we was anchoring, did you get a look at the beach north side of the river? Right in front of a few cottages among a stand of pines?"

He frowned at me, but he nodded.

"There's a road back of them pines what leads down to the sea and connects with the road around the town. It's out of the line of sight from the wharves because the river kinks as it meets the sea. We're anchored far enough into the river's outfall that if you launch the boats from the ship, the current from the river will take them almost all the way to the beach, no oars squeaking in rowlocks."

He caught on right quick.

"So you go up the marsh road, meet the man with the price of the trip, have him get the supercargo organized, take them around the back of the town in the dark, cross the bridge, and straight on to the beach," he says, like he'd just had the idea all by himself.

"No bridge. The river's way wider up stream." I says. "Ferry. Flat bottomed barge, big enough for a wagon with four horses."

"Ferryman?" he asks.

"Do it yerself with ropes. Done it more'n often, taking sailors to and from them cottages I told you about -- the ones what we could see from the ship."

He looked at me crooked, like he was wondering if I had something up me sleeve. I knew that look. He was changing his mind about me, wondering if I was the mark he'd taken me for so far, or whether I might be fixing to make him the mark.

"Who's in the cottages?"

"That's where the sailors 'friends live."

He give me a quick look and nodded. He'd decided I was a little cunning and maybe a bit gullible, but on his side.

"Time to go," he said quietly.

We was no sooner standing than two important-looking men came through the door. They was still wearing their Sunday best, but they had swords strapped around their middles. They looked the place over, and beckoned the publican to them. While the taller of the two checked off names on a list, the other arranged for a little liquid bribery.

"A round for these fine fellows on me, Innkeeper. My men will spend the night here." Then he dropped his voice and spoke in the publican's ear, but I heard him clear. "After the one round, no more, unless I say so."

Markab headed for the door, with me looking humble and seamanlike at his port shoulder. I'll say this for him, he could keep his cool. He walked right up to the two men in charge, his hand out, like they was old friends.

"Gentlemen," he says. "Didn't I see you in church today? And here you are, doing your duty as stalwart leaders of the town."

An 'what could they do in front of their men but start shaking his hand and calling him "captain." So he goes on buttering them up.

"Gentlemen, I must return to my ship, but should you require any assistance in defending your fine community, you can call on me and my ship's company."

O 'course, that meant that they had to say a whole lot of words that boiled down to "Thanks, but no thanks, we can handle it," and by the time we'd gone around the politeness buoy a couple of times, we were out of the pub, and heading down to the wharves, stepping aside for a few late arrivals to the town's little army. By a big slice of unearned luck, I was in the shadows, trailing along a little astern of Markab's port shoulder when I saw that one of the recruits was none other than me old Da. What with me wearing me nice new officer-like clothes and standing in Markab's lee, and with Da's fearsome thirst what was never so strong as when someone else might be paying, he never so much as glimpsed me. As he went in the door, I saw him dig his elbow into the fellow beside him so as to show him what he had tucked under his jacket. Lamplight gleamed on the barrel of some kind of handgun or pistol. At that moment, me innards took a notion to turn over. I knew that guns were rare, expensive, deadly, and because the ammunition was old, unpredictable. Sort of like me Da. Put the two of them together and trouble was getting ready to happen. I took a deep breath and kept moving. I wasn't about to share what I'd seen with anyone, least of all the master.

When we was around a corner and out of sight in the shadows, Markab gave me a little box of fire-sticks and a stump of candle for signalling, and we told each other goodbye. I was keen to get away from anywhere near me Da, and Markab wanted to get back to the ship ready to be gone and hull down if the whole plan got scuppered. He walked back to the wharves, when he was well out of sight, I took another track I knew around the south edge of town, clear of the pretend soldiers, what I had no intention of being anywhere near.

And now after all that talk, I needs me liquid rations, what those good women who look after me are so parsimonious with. Join me?

Four

Where was I? Yeah. On me way around the town, taking me time so's not to run into nobody till I met up with with the supercargo. The more-or-less secret track led around the steep and cliffy south side of the hill, right close to where it weren't a good idea to put up any more houses, and where most folk don't go for fear of falling off, 'cause the path's ragged in spots, which is why boys and spry men like it. It were too late for me to meet anyone, and anyway, it was one of those spots where if you pass someone, you pretend not to notice, and keep on going.

Seaport town. There's always stuff what people want that ain't available in regular daytime stores.

Halfway up and along, I looked back at the harbour to where *Wetfoot* lay waiting. Her anchor light was glowing yellowy-white, and beyond her I could see dim gleams from the cottages of the sailors 'friends. Closer in, a few fish boats were rafted together alongside one of the wharves, a light moving around where someone was finishing up a long day or getting ready for an early start tomorrow. I wondered if I should be worrying about fishermen catching on to Markab's and my plan, but I decided that they was likely more interested in fishing.

I sat there listening to the night wind whispering cool enough so's I was glad of me nice almost-new blue jacket, watching the dark seep up out of the east, turning the water black. I waited until the moon rose and I had enough light to make me way slowly south and west to where the marsh road met the highway near where it crossed the stream. All the time, I was trying to make up me mind how to meet and greet the passengers. I knew roughly where they should be, and I had a password, but I reckoned they was likely to be edgy, and nervous folk with knives can make mistakes.

As it turned out, I didn't need to worry. Some time before midnight, I reached the road and started south. I heard me heels echo on the little bridge afore I saw it, and a short bit later, I was into where the pine forest was on either side. It was right dark under the trees, so I slowed down, feeling me way with me feet, stopping every few paces to listen. First time, wind in trees. Second time, same again. Third time, a tiny scream, cut off. Some little critter turning into an owl's dinner. Two more stops, and I heard something jingling what I knew weren't no forest sound. Another few steps, listen again, and there was an on-and-off thudding sound mixed in with the jinglin', and I knew I was hearing horses what hadn't been taken out of their harnesses for the night. I was bent over in a patch of moonlight with me nose close to the ground, feeling with me fingers for where the horses had left the road, when low down under the branches I caught a gleam of a fire. I was just about to straighten up, when a whisper stopped me dead.

"What's the good word?"

Something poked me in the back, so I held right still.

"One chance. Get it right."

"*Tidewalker*," I whispered back. "The ship's name is *Tidewalker*."

Then I was looking straight into a little candle lantern held at eye level. It weren't all that bright, but after a few hours picking me way by moon and starlight, I couldn't see nothing of the man who held it. He looked me over, taking in me nice new nautical rig, and he grunted.

"You have a name?"

"Angel."

He grunted again, this time like if had it been some other time and place, he might'a laughed.

"Follow me, Angel."

I stumbled along behind him, catching me toes in roots and rocks. He led me to the fire I'd glimpsed, which was in the middle of a clearing. At first, I thought there was nobody there, until I saw a hunched-over shape of a big, square man sitting on a log. He had a huge head of hair and a thick beard. Bushy isn't enough of a word for that beard. It was a forest hanging down over a chest big enough for two men. But it was the eyes that held me. Bright in the firelight, shiny-black. They didn't blink.

"His name's Angel. He knew the password."

The big man did not even nod. I was still waiting for his eyelids to move when he spoke.

"Are you a righteous or an evil angel?"

He spoke quiet, but his voice boomed like his big chest was an open barrel. I was impressed, but I'd had enough righteousness for the day.

"Able Angel is me name. And what do I call you?" I says, making me voice officer-like and not noticeably humble,

"I am Abner. And you will lead us down to the harbour and your ship."

"No."

He blinked. His head turned a point or two to starboard, and his eyes got narrower.

"Why?"

"'Cause the town knows you're here and planning to arrive by the marsh road. They're expecting a raiding party. They caught some poor feller who must have told them you was armed and dangerous. They don't know you've got women and children."

"Joel."

"I didn't hear a name for you to thank, and from the way they were talkin', Joel is beyond thankin'."

"Thanking?"

"For telling them where to jump you. Makes it possible for me to take you another way. If'n the rest of yer party can get on the road just about right now, with no lights."

His shiny black eyes kept staring at me. First off, it were disturbin'. Then when he didn't say nothing, I got to thinking he was wondering whether to trust me, cause I knew the way, and he didn't. What I'd told him was more than just a change in his plans. It must have crossed his mind that maybe I was only telling part of the truth about the reception committee, and that my job was to lead him and his crew straight into it.

Everything he'd said and hadn't said told me that he was a man who needed to be in charge of every damn thing, and at that moment, he wasn't, and he was doing his best to hide it. All he knew was that I was dressed like a fairly important sailor, and that I'd answered with the right ship's name. It occurred to me that he might be wondering if I would still be singing the same song after someone had worked me over a bit. That idea weren't comforting. So I squatted down on me heels with the fire between us, and our heads on the same level. I looked into his shiny, black, unblinking eyes, and spoke plain and direct, like the officer and gen'leman I so surely wasn't.

"Abner, let me tell you what I propose."

For the first time, his eyes blinked.

"When you come out of the woods onto the road again, there's the marsh road to starboard -- on your right hand. We're going past it, around the back of the town, along the road that's in the lee of the hill what's topped by the church. We start out going north and then curl around eastwards, until we come to the river. A couple of hours walk for a man, more if there's women and children. There's a do-it-yourself ferry big enough for four horses and a wagon, with room for a couple dozen people if they scrunch up close. We take the trip across -- it's not much more than twice as far as you could throw a stone -- and then follow the road on the other side to the beach, where me captain will have boats to take you aboard W...*Tidewalker*."

For a few heartbeats he looked at me, and I looked back.

"I understand," he said, and his words carried a lot of freight. He was relieved, I could tell. So much so, that I knew I could go on asking questions.

"Abner, tell me, where are your … er… crew? We have no time to go looking for and rounding up stragglers. And they have to be quiet."

"They're close. And they know how to do that."

"The women and children, too?"

His big head went up and down.

"The family will be on the road soon enough. See to it, Jonas."

The feller who'd guided me to the fire nodded, the orange light from the flames showing me a big hooky nose with a face around it that was all angles and shadows. He nodded, and disappeared into the dark. I could hear small rustling noises and occasional whispers. Soon I glimpsed people moving out from the trees and bushes into the edges of the firelight, what there was of it, and on through the trees. Someone got the horses pulling a heavy wagon towards the road. Abner picked up a candle lantern, got slowly to his feet, and waved a big hand at me to follow him. Behind us, I heard hissing as they dowsed the fire.

Eventually, they was all of a piece and on the road waiting to get started. I joined Jonas, Abner's lead hand, and we went down one side of the line and up the other, counting by the light of Abner's little lantern. I made it five men besides Abner and me, twelve or so women, about a dozen boys and girls, all of them somewhat more than six years, none of them more'n twelve or so. In the dark, whatever they was wearing looked mostly grey, with a few even harder-to-see in black. The young ones was bunched together around the women, on account of them being ma's. A few of the older children were helping out, but most was standing clear in twos and threes. All of the girls wore shawls and kept their heads down. Some of the older ones were holding the hands of the littler ones. The boys wore caps pulled low. I couldn't see faces, but they all was all standing quietly, like they was too tired and sleepy and scared to do anything else. As Jonas came past, counting, a couple of them shied away, like they was staying out of reach, same as I used to do when me Da was around.

When we'd got back to the wagon and horses at the head of the line, a movement caught me eye. On the tailgate, back of a pile of stuff what I couldn't see 'cause it were under a tarpaulin and in the dark, was a girl dangling her feet, wearing a dress that had been white once, with a baby on her knees all wrapped up in a blanket. Her hair gleamed in the light, but I couldn't make out the colour beyond that it weren't black. She was singing real soft in the little one's ear. Jonas took one step in front of me and clipped her one upside her head.

In the light of his lantern I saw her hair fly up, pale and shiny, and her eyes flashed white. She gasped, and slid off the tailgate, the baby cuddled close to her on one skinny hip. There was something odd about the two of them, because she weren't old enough to be no ma, that's for sure.

I opened me mouth to ask why she couldn't ride on the wagon, but Jonas got in his whisper first.

"Let her walk. Maybe we'll lose her along the way. She's no good to anyone, nor the kid, neither. Sure to die soon, anyway. Don't know why Abner let her tag along after the mother croaked."

Well, that struck me as rare mean and nasty, but short of knifing the bastard and rolling his body into the ditch, there weren't nothing I could do, and besides, the girl and the baby had disappeared into the shadows. So we went on to join the wagon and horses where Abner was waiting to give the word to get started, which, soon as he had climbed aboard the wagon, he did.

That were the beginning of a long, slow walk around the edges of the town. It turned out to be the longest night I can recall; longer than any night watch I ever stood, then or later, 'cause I remember all of it, not like at sea, where the waves rub the details smooth, and one night watch is much the same as the last. I was out in front of the horses, holding a dim lantern that showed Abner just enough of the road for him to keep the wagon on it. Behind me, I heard the horses' hooves softly thudding onto the grass strip down the middle, the wagon creaking, the occasional whimper or whisper from the women and kids, and from time to time a muttered curse from the men what were strung out behind, keeping the whole sorry procession on the move.

As the night wore on, I remember grappling with something new to me: I was split up and down the middle of me own thoughts, with the two bits tugging in different directions. Never happened to me before. Up to then, it had been me looking out for me, 'cause sure as night follows day, nobody else did -- except Al and Smitty, and they was dead. Y'see, looking out for me had been so time-and-me-consuming, I didn't have nothing left over for anyone else, not even the memories of poor old Al and Smitty, who both deserved more than the deep six. So that was why it was all so strange to me as I walked the night away, followed by a couple dozen folks I'd not even heard of a day earlier. I just couldn't understand why I had this great big squirmy feeling that I should do something about the skinny girl and the baby she was looking after like she had no thought for her own self. And at the very same time as I was thinking I should do something about her, I was also telling meself to get the job done like the Master had ordered and I had helped plan, and never mind the supercargo beyond delivering them, or at least most of them. But as I was walking and thinking, I wasn't at all that happy with what I'd seen. I was also more than a piece worried by what I hadn't seen. Stuff like what had come before, like the ma dying and them keeping the skinny girl on, but not taking proper care of her.

Now you got to know that I was least happy with Markab, him being ready to cut and run from his agreement the moment the deal looked like it were getting dodgy. With Markab, I had the sass to come up with an idea that would keep him in the game. With Abner, I had no such lever or lucky idea to make him to show some consideration for the girl and the baby. So I kept on walkin', hopin', and arguing with myself to no good conclusion. Abner had the wagon, he'd put Jonas in charge of the rank and file strung out behind. I wasn't going to convert Jonas to me way of thinking, and no way I could go over his head to Abner. Each time I circled around the same uncomfortable thoughts, I kept on coming back to those wide blue eyes on the skinny girl who was looking after what must have been her baby brother or sister.

As the sky brightened with the false dawn, we started down the slope that led to the river. Mist hung low to the water's edge, so that we could only see to the end of the ferry dock. Right where the ferry wasn't.

"It ain't here," said Jonas. "Now you got a problem."

He sounded like he was pleased. I ignored him and began hauling on the recovery line while the horses' hooves clopped and thudded on the wood of the dock. I could feel Jonas and Abner watching me, but I paid them no mind, 'cause I could feel the ferry swinging across the river towards me. All I had to do was maintain a steady pressure, and the current would do the work. But I wasn't going to tell them that, nor that I was wondering why the ferry was on the other side, and coming to the conclusion that the sailors must have been so keen and the sailors' friends so willing that they'd all decided to make a night of it. Then the ugly old square-ended barge of a ferry ghosted out of the mist and bumped against the dock, and I was busy getting the ramp down and the horses and the people aboard without no feet nor fingers getting squashed. But while I was doing me fussing around, I was looking for the skinny girl, and not seeing her nowhere. Finally, as I got the ramp up and the folks standing clear, I leaned on the big steering oar to shove her bow out so's the current got on her port side to push her away from the dock and angle her across the river into the mist. While I could still see, I kept me eyes on the dock, hoping that there would be the skinny girl, but I didn't see nothing but ripples on the water and the black wood of the dock getting fuzzier in the mist as we swung away.

I decided she must have got lost along the way. I pictured her in me mind's eye, limping along behind, falling, and not being able to get up. And I was ashamed that I wasn't there when that was happening, and guilty that I'd pushed off in the ferry before seeing whether I couldn't do anything about her. It left me with a hole in meself, 'cause I hadn't done nothing when I might'a, and the more I knew I wasn't going back to make it better, the worse I felt. So I leaned on the steering oar and looked at me feet while the ferry swung away from the dock and the mist thickened around us.

Then I heard horses' hooves on the dock, invisible ashore, and a lot of voices talking at the same time.

"That was close," said Abner softly, turning to look back over the load on the wagon. The women and children started whispering.

"Quiet," he said

And they were -- just like that. If I hadn't had so much to do, I'd 'a been wonderstruck, but I was right busy with the steering oar, trying to get that barge of a ferry across the river as quick as I could. It was a good thing Abner had silenced his people, because otherwise I might not have heard a shout from the dock we had just left.

"Angel!"

You can bet I swung around right quick, but not before I saw Abner point at me, and all four of his men push past the women to get to me. I very briefly considered taking a header over the side before things could get worse, but then we all heard another shout, this time through the mist from the other side of the river.

"I'm here, and we got em!" yelled a voice I knew right away was me Da.

"Good work, Angel," came the first voice, and then louder. "Right, you in the ferry. You're stuck. Go on to the other side and you'll get shot. Give up. We're going to haul you back over here."

"No you won't," I said, and cut the recovery lines, letting the ends drop into the water.

Abner's men were almost on me, so I climbed over the top of the wagon, talking as I went.

"Don't fret, Abner. It's me Da they're talking to. Him and me don't get along. 'Sides, I got a plan."

He must have caught on, or maybe he was just surprised, 'cause he let me slide past him down onto the whippletree a'tween the horses, and down into the space between the horses' heads and the strong post that was the belay for the anchor rope what kept the ferry head-to-current so's it could swing like a pendulum back and forth across the river.

I got me knife out and started to cut the hawser, but it was thicker than me arm, fog-wet and bar-taught. Still, I gave it me best, even though the mist was lifting and the daylight coming on, and I knew the folks ashore would soon figger out what I was up to, and start shooting. So there I was, bent over, trying to make myself small, when I felt a hand grab me shoulder. I didn't even lift me head to swear.

"Bugger off, numb ..." I began.

"Out of my way, Angel. Back to your oar."

It were Abner, and he had an axe. I ducked clear, and as I started back the way I'd come, I heard the axe thunk into the rope. Then something like an angry bee zinged past me head, and I heard the bang. I didn't stop, and Abner's men had the sense to hunker down below the barge's wooden sides, where they got the women and young ones to do the same. That was good, 'cause they weren't getting in me way or trying to nobble me, but on the other hand, when I arrived at the steering oar, there I was alone and standing up, as much a target as I had been at the other end.

Another bang, and one of the horses screamed and started kicking, but that wasn't my worry, because I saw the water wasn't flowing past the ferry anymore. Abner and his axe had done the job, and we were being carried by the current, floating down the river and out into the harbour. Just as I was thinking that we were probably out of range of me Da's pistol, the dawn mist cleared away like someone had planned it all along. They could see us, we could see them, and when I took a quick look for Wetfoot, there she was, boats in the falls, getting ready to pick us up from the beach where we weren't, and weren't going to be, neither. Out of the corner of me eye, I saw someone up at the bow on anchor watch start waving and jumpin', and there was a faint yell of "boat ahoy!"

Behind us, men were shouting at each other from both sides of the river -- a sure recipe for nothing happening for a while. But they weren't important anymore, so long as I got the next bit right, that is.

I leaned on the steering oar, shoving it as far as I could to port, or what I hoped would be port, when I got the scabby sided barge turned around so's me and the steering oar was both in the stern. Slowly, she swung around until we were drifting sideways into the harbour, losing speed and steerage way as the fresh water of the river mixed with the sea. I levered down on the loom of the oar to pick it out of the water, swing it back and take another bite at turning the blunt-ended box of a boat around, but the sweep was old, long and water-heavy, so it caught on the surface.

"Could use some help here," I sung out.

"Help him Jonas," said Abner.

His voice was no more than what a feller would use to call for a beer in a tavern, but it were better than a full-on shout, 'cause it got the lean and rangy fellow to me side quicker than it takes me to tell yer. So we pushed and shoved together until we had to ease off 'cause the oar was bending something frightenin'. But we brought her around and heading roughly at *Wetfoot*, where now I could see signs that they was beginning to catch the drift of what we were about.

For a while, it looked like we were going on past and heading out to sea, then what was left of the current took a twirl that carried us so far sideways that I feared we'd end up draped across *Wetfoot's* bow. So did the folks aboard. Some of them had heaving lines to pull us close, some had boat hooks and fenders to push us away before we did damage, 'cause that barge of a ferry was a heavy, waterlogged tub, built to last by folk who were interested in strong, not swift, an' least of all nimble.

Well, by now you guessed that we made it, and handsomely. We slid past the bowsprit, caught the lines they threw us, and laid alongside like it were something we'd all practiced for years. Soon the supercargo were swarming up the scrambling nets, and the crew had the mizzen gaff rigged as a davit to hoist the horses and wagon on board. I stayed in the ferry to encourage the folks to climb, and then to place the slings under the wagon. When I looked at the horses, wondering how I'd deal with them, there was Abner, getting them out of harness like he did it every day.

Up went the wagon, and then back down onto the deck between the two after masts. Then we went to work on the horses, and that was something else to see how Abner calmed them down, even the one what me Da had shot. Up they went, their big eyes rolling and their legs dangling like rag dolls. And then Abner looked at me, and I looked back, and we both grinned, like two men who know they've done a right fine job. Then we slipped the lines and climbed up the scrambling net to the ship's deck in time to hear the Master order the anchor broken clear of the bottom, the main and jib hoisted, and the barge left to drift wherever it wanted to go. I heard distant cursing from the shore, and very satisfying that was, too.

I was enjoying the moment, looking around at everyone but me workin', pleased with how they were taking more than a few looks at me new clothes, and casting me practiced nautical eye at how they were securing the horses and wagon where they'd readied space ahead of the mainmast for deck cargo, right next to where they'd fixed up a makeshift pen for the horses, when I saw the edge of the tarpaulin lifted up by a thin arm, and two heads looking out.

I was beside the wagon in a heartbeat. It was the skinny girl. She had copper-coloured hair, and her eyes were blue-green like the open sea in sunlight. She was having a bit of a job getting to the deck with the little one hanging on to her, so I made meself useful. I took hold of the baby, and felt at once that she was bigger than I'd thought, and as plump as the girl was skinny. She didn't smell too good, and she sure didn't want to be held by no strange man, but she didn't cry. The moment I set her on her feet, she had one hand holding the skinny girl's dress and the other one in her mouth, looking at me through blue-grey eyes over her fat little fist.

I was that pleased, I laughed out loud.

Five

So I was telling you about how I got Abner and his folks to *Wetfoot*, now I have to tell you what I found out on the voyage to where we landed them. O' course, most of the time I had me duties to perform, watches to keep, orders to follow, and a few orders to give, too. Markab was as good as his word and moved me on up to be leading hand of the green and keen, meaning that I was in charge of the youngest members of the crew, what had volunteered under circumstances not too much different from me own, nigh on five years earlier when I went aboard *Stella*. I suppose it was a good idea, 'cause I wasn't trying to boss men old enough to be me father or young enough to be resentful that I'd been given a leg up past them, but it did mean that I was the youngest and newest member of the other lead hands, and they weren't any too happy to have someone they regarded as a jumped-up young sprog from another ship becoming a member of their exalted comp'ny, and with a share now, as well as a wage. I messed with them at the noon meal every day, but it wasn't an occasion involving friendly banter and cheerful, witty bonhomie. 'Stead, they was all looking to find me wanting and then to catch me out, mostly because I wasn't one of them. The leading hand of the starboard watch was me tormentor-in-chief. Enif by name and nosy by nature, he kept on trying to get me talking about me family. Me "humble origins" is what he called it. He was forever trying to catch me doing something wrong from the moment I came aboard *Wetfoot*. And o'course, this ever-so-kind-and-continuous attention primed the rest of the crew to think I had me promotion for landlubbing reasons only a whisker different from serious brown nosing, that fine line being the way I'd brought the ferry to the ship, which none of them could fault.

Yer probably thinking that I passed me spare time chatting up the best looking of the women passengers. No such luck. We'd no sooner got under way when Markab called the whole ship's company together and told us that we could stay strictly away from the women and girls, or feed the fishes. He said it so's everyone believed he wasn't foolin'. He spoke like he shoved men over the side at dawn on the first day of every second week before repairing to his cabin to eat a hearty breakfast. Abner stood beside him and nodded his head like he thought this was a splendid idea what he'd be pleased to lend a hand with.

Abner and the master put the supercargo off limits to the crew because they wanted none of the shenanigans that might be expected when quite a few females get mixed up with a shipload of sailors what hadn't been ashore in a long while. It made sense, too: any fooling around would be quickly followed by fights involving Abner's men, then among the sailors, maybe even among the women, too.

So all the crew saw of the women and children was when they was let up on the foredeck for some fresh air, so long as it was gentle weather. That was when I saw the skinny girl with the chubby little girl-baby taking the air. The little one was going everywhere at the run, disappearing behind legs and bodies, followed by the girl making sure she didn't go over the side, her bright hair tied high on the back of her head and flipping up as she moved. The two of them were weaving in and out of the grown-ups' feet, the little one giggling and both of them getting frowned down on by the men who had herded their women and girls into groups over which they watched like drakes with their ducks.

I was making meself busy while watching and grinning when the skinny girl near to tripped Jonas -- the man who'd been right nasty to her when all she wanted was to ride on the wagon. Even though we were on a broad reach in light airs, with *Wetfoot* as steady as any three-masted schooner can be, the lubber had no sea legs at all. His first little stagger turned into such an arm-waving jig-step that he only escaped taking a header into the salt-chuck by winding himself around the foremast stays. It was enough to make the ship's cat laugh. When that's what just about everyone did, Jonas lost what'cher call his composure, and headed off after the skinny girl and the little one, shouting -- well, shouting stuff that shouldn't never be said around women and their children, still less at them. I had heard it all before, and learned to say it meself when I was a nipper, until Al reformed me, bless him. He set great store in being polite and never using bad words, and I suppose it rubbed off on me, special after he'd told me I could forget coming back for more book-learning if I didn't foreswear swearin', which I always thought was a confusing way of putting it into words ...

Just a moment, where was I?

Right. Jonas roaring around the foredeck, chasing the chubby little one, who was giggling as she ran down the narrow bit of deck between the forward cabin and the port rail, towards me. I stepped out right sharp and scooped her up, still gigglin'. With me arms full of soft little toddler, I saw Jonas catch up with the skinny girl and give her a shove that sent her spinning towards me. Well, what with her grabbing me spare hand, and me getting an elbow around the mizzen halyards without letting go of the little one, somehow we all stayed aboard. It were a closer thing for Jonas. If only I'd stuck me foot out in a quiet and cunning way, life might'a been different for me -- and a lot of other people besides. But I didn't, and he stayed aboard by falling headlong, flat on his face into the scuppers where the ship's rail saved him from the salt chuck.

While he was getting to his feet and pulling himself together, the three of us unwound ourselves from the halyards and each other. The skinny girl steadied herself against the cabin and grabbed the little one's hand. The other fat little hand flew up to her face so she could shove her thumb into her mouth, and she looked up at me over her fist so steady that her big, round, blue-grey eyes didn't even blink.

Jonas clambered to his feet and lurched towards me, elbows out, fists ready. I'd seen how long his arms were when he was dancing his near-to-falling-over jig, so I let him come towards me, shoved the two girls astern of the mast, where there was plenty to hang on to and then stepped back to the lee side, out of his reach. Jonas' feet still thought he was on dry land, so his next step towards me was off-balance. I nearly took a poke at that big nose, then thought better of it, tempting though it was. So I stood still, lots of seawater rushing past a short step away, and the mizzen boom for me to lean against, in what you call a negligent posture of calculated inattention, while he white-knuckled the shrouds and stared down at the water he'd so nearly fallen into.

"Jonas," I said real quiet, like I was thinking great thoughts. "Only a letter away from Jonah. Now, what do you think every sailor aboard would say if I told them that someone named Jonah accidentally went over the side? They'd cheer, that's what."

"Superstitious twaddle…" he began, trying to sneer, but I cut him off.

"Maybe. But aboard and afloat, we've been believing it since old Holy shoved the first and unluckiest Jonah into the belly of a whale. An 'ever since, Jonah is the name sailors use for unlucky men what nobody wants as a shipmate -- or even a supercargo. You should believe me, 'cause they will."

I paused, reflective-like. He didn't say nothing, but his long arms had dropped.

"So what is your name, anyway?" I asked, and then not waiting for an answer, went on. "Oh, I remember. Harry. Harry, If I was you, I'd lose that other name what sounds so much like Jonah, at least when you're here on deck where the sailors are."

I could see he was taking it in. His fists were hands again, and he was using them to steady himself against the cabin.

"And one more thing, Harry …"

He looked a question at me. He was not happy, but he was thinking more about what I'd said than about how much he'd like to have me down on the deck and thumping me with them big fists. So like they say in books, I pursued me advantage.

"You so much as look crooked at either these two girls, and you will certainly find out how easy accidents can happen to big-booted lubbers. An' you have to know that nobody is going to be surprised, now you've shown everyone that you can't hardly stay upright when it's calm as it ever gets. Now get along for'ard with the rest of the supercargo, and I'll see the children back to where they belong."

So there I was, talking fancy, leaning against the boom telling meself how smart I was to get the upper hand on a man old enough to be me uncle, if I had one. Pride, as old Al loved to say, goeth before a fall.

Markab and Abner appeared around the mainmast and the master lit right into me. You can bet that me casual posture turned swiftly into an attitude of respect, maybe with even a little bit of a cringe.

"And just what part of my orders didn't you understand?"

Smited, I thought to meself. Do something good for someone, and what do you get? Smited. But then Abner spoke up like nobody in the entire ship's company would have dreamed of doing.

"Captain Markab, perhaps I may intervene. Your man Angel seems to have averted what might have been a tragic end for two children."

For a moment, Markab looked like he was ready to push Abner into the sea, but he recovered quickly, took a breath and let it go slowly, taking his temper with it.

"Very well. You may have a point. What do you suggest?"

Abner smiled. That is, his beard and moustache wiggled like maybe his lips were smiling underneath all that hair.

"Your man is Angel by name and angel by nature, it seems. Why not make him my family's guardian angel, at least as long as we're aboard your ship."

Markab gave a little snort of a grunt.

"You heard him, Angel. You're now protector of women and children. Any one of them goes over the side, you'll follow."

Well, let me tell you I went from cringing to chuffed in an instant. I snapped out an "At your command!" and touched me forehead, looking under me hand to watch the two of them turn their backs on me seamanlike response and return to the quarterdeck, where they should have been the whole time.

So then I looked around at the skinny girl, hoping for at least a smile, or maybe a word or two of appreciation for me taking her part. But no. She came out from behind the mast, walked up to me and hit me in the chest with her little fist. It weren't no love tap, neither: she put all she had into it. Smited again, and by a girl with a little one holding onto her other hand.

"Stupid sailor," she said. "Now old man Abner is going to be watching us."

"Better him than that bastard Jonas," says I. Then, like I was doing me duty as the Master told me, "Now let's get the two of you back with the rest of them."

I took the little one's other hand, who gave me the big grin I had been hoping to get from the skinny girl.

"What's your name?" I asked, ignoring the girl. The little one took her thumb out of her mouth just long enough to say "Sally," and then stuffed it back in again.

"So, what's your sister's name?"

Out came the thumb. "She's Michael." And back it went.

"Michael? That's a boy's name," I said.

The skinny girl spoke up for herself.

"No it's not. Our mother gave me the name. She's dead."

That brought me up all standing. Her words were so blunt, so short, so final.

"So Abner's your father?" I asked.

"You are stupid, aren't you? You saw Jason toss us off the gun wagon. Do you think a real father would let him knock us about like that?"

I didn't say nothing because we were almost back to where the women were trying to keep the young ones from falling over the side, but the words" gun wagon" made me curious.

I got me chance for a closer look at what was under the tarpaulin around dawn the next morning. I'd waited until the end of the night watch, when it was just getting light, and everyone but me was half-asleep. I got meself two buckets of fresh water, and snuck up the midships companionway, around the lee side of the mainmast to where the wagon had been secured to pad-eyes in the deck, athwartships and alongside the livestock pen. Two sleepy, hungry and very thirsty horses were right glad to see me. So while they was sucking up water, I loosened the tie-down on the back end of the tarpaulin and took a peek underneath. What I saw was a waist-high, solid stack of grey boxes with rope handles at the ends, most of them about the size and shape that would hold a man's leg. They were well roped down to the wagon, and all had numbers and letters on them, too smudged to read. I was just about to climb in for a better look-see, when I heard someone at the other end of the wagon.

"Hi, there," I said, making a show of straightening the canvass and checking the holding-down ropes what kept the wagon in place. "Feeding yer horses?" I added, when I saw the rest of him. He was a bulky, square man, not much older than me. I saw big shoulders, big arms and big hands what at that moment were carrying two tubs of feed.

A round face with a thatch of brown hair looked over the wagon's load. We exchanged names: his was Matthew, Matt for short.

"You bring them the water? Thanks."

"No strain. You got a shovel there? Skipper won't like what yer horses is doing to the deck."

Matt pulled out two, and we shovelled. When we were done, I sluiced down the deck with a bucket on the end of a line, and we stood and watched the horses until they were finished drinking and eating. He picked up the empty tubs and slid them under the driver's seat alongside the feed sacks.

"Settler's tools?" I asked casual-like, jerking me head towards the boxes under the tarpaulin.

"Near two hundred rifles, along with bullets. Beautiful. Oiled, wrapped, with wax poured solid into each box."

I nodded, trying to look unimpressed, but he guessed that I'd never seen anything but the occasional rifle or handgun either made by a local smith, or more often a rust-pitted relic.

"It's a shame, really," Matt went on, eager to amaze some dumb sailor. "So much destroyed, blown up and broken by the Fresh Start crazies, trying to get rid of everything left over from Before."

"People believe some right strange stuff," says I, encouraging him.

"You got that right. Special when they're dying."

"Dying from what?"

"The Rot. Plague. The Fresh Starters all got it. They were the ones that weren't dead when everyone else was. Maybe they thought they wouldn't catch the Rot. Maybe they knew they were going to die sooner or later, and didn't want nobody outliving them. Maybe they were crazed by all they'd seen. Who knows what went on in their heads, and I sure don't want to. They went about tearing down and burning everything they could. They destroyed factories and warehouses and farms. Abner says that when the soldiers and police tried to stop them, then they got the Rot, too. So some of them became Fresh Starters as well. And I guess they were the best blower-uppers and fire-starters of all."

"Didn't happen around where I was," I said.

"Me neither, leastways, not much, though I seen the edges of it, and it weren't pretty. I come from where most folks were right enough, even when people were dying just over the next ridge. Perhaps they thought nothing bad would happen to them. But Abner knew. He saw how things were going, so he collected up the six — now five — of us, along with healthy women and children. And now he's taking us to the place where we're going to start again, where it's safe. We are the new beginning: *in hope, in faith, in loyalty, and in peace.*"

Matt had been telling his tale like it was one he'd told before, but then he said the last few words the way people do when they pray together out loud, kind of chanting what they've been heard so many times they think it's their own idea. It gave me a confused, crawly feeling up the back of me neck to hear him talking so cheerful and proud, right next to a wagon-load of guns. I didn't say nothin'. Sure, one or two might be useful for shooting game or keeping the varmints down, but why did Abner need more guns than he had grown men and women? How did that fit into a new beginning in faith, hope, and peace?

Then it hit me. The guns were payment to Markab. An' the idea of that treacherous bastard owning guns made me guts turn over. I already told yer how I felt about me Da having one ancient and unreliable gun in his fist even before he had a shot at blowing me away with it, so the idea of Markab having dozens of guns got me mind in a twist.

So now, before I tell yer what changed things for me, I figger it's time for that pint you smuggled past the little woman that makes me life miserable for lack of the good things. Cider eh? Last year's batch? Made it yourself? Good for you, lass.

Six

After I was put in charge of the supercargo as well as me other duties, I spent a fair piece of me not particularly generous allotment of free time keeping the young ones from going over the side, making sure they all got their fair share of the food and drink, and politely answering questions from the mums with wise and seamanlike answers like, "Yes, mum, the ship is s'posed to lean away from the wind; don't worry about it."

As the only one of the *Wetfoot's* crew what was allowed forward of the foremast, I didn't have to be told not to fool about. At first, I spent me time chasing down wandering little-uns, and impressing upon the young lads that if they fooled around with the sheets and halyards they'd live to regret it. It was like being a big brother, or an uncle, or something like that. I was soon explaining to them how the sails work, or showing them how to tie knots. That fascinated them, girls and boys the both.

I started off with bowline on a bight, which is real easy but looks like magic if'n you do it quick. When that got their attention, I asked the old question, "What's a good knot?" and sure enough one of the boys said, "A knot that doesn't come undone," which meant that I could give me smart-arsed smile and say, "Half right. A knot what don't come undone — until you want it to." And then I had me bit of fun with chain hitches that let go when you pull the end, like a couple girls knew from their stitchin'. Then I showed them a bunch of useful knots and finished up with a tom-fool's knot, what you use for tying people up. It's a knot that's all in the way you make it happen, and, 'cause everyone looks at the rope 'stead of the way you hold it, they don't figger out how to do it.

The mums watched, and a couple of them thanked me for keeping the young ones amused, but not a single one of them said anything about where they had come from, why they were aboard, or where they were going. I guessed that fear, pain, loss, and just plain ignorance was all part of it, but what made me puzzled was that in the present, the here and now aboard *Wetfoot*, they would talk to me but not to each other -- when I was around, anyway. A bunch of women and children with no gossip: it didn't seem possible. I exercised me undoubted charm and amazing good looks, especially when the men weren't within hearing, which was most of the time, but it made no difference.

You remember how I told you that when Abner said "Quiet," they all obeyed him, even faster than a seaman jumping to the Master's orders? The man had powers. I'd felt them right from when we met in the forest, but somehow the trick hadn't worked on me. We'd worked together like shipmates in that lumbering barge of a ferry, first to cut it loose, then to offload the supercargo, the wagon and the horses. We'd trusted each other, and we'd got the job done without the need for talk. He hadn't ordered me around, like his man Jason tried to do.

I felt somehow comfortable with Abner, like I'd known him for ever and respected him even longer. And that's how I figgered it must be why the women and young folks behaved. It troubled me a bit that for the women there was something that wasn't fear, but was real close to it. A mum had only to say, "Abner wants you to …" for her daughters or sons to straighten right up and do as they were told. It worked every time — except on the skinny girl with the boy's name.

That soft, shrinking silence what hung over all of them was water off a gull's back to her. I could see it in the way she looked after little Sally, keeping her away from the other mums and their children, often by calling her in a voice three times louder than the whispers and murmurs the rest of them used. She wore the same long skirts as the mums, once white, now grey, and she had the same kind of homespun shawl to cover her mostly white, long-sleeve blouse like the others, but I could spot her in the crowd the moment I got going each day, whether I was getting them up on the fo'c'sle deck in the wind or back down into the tween-decks to be all squashed in together. It was easy to see her, and it wouldn't have been any easier if she had been wearing bright red with feathers in her copper-coloured hair, which most of the time she didn't cover with her shawl, the way the rest of the women and girls did. And if I kept track of her the whole time, so did the mums and the other girls. They left her alone, and watched her out of the corner of their eyes, like they were waiting for something serious bad to happen to her; and though they didn't want to be part of it, they sure were counting on watching it happen.

After a little more than a week at sea, we made landfall. As we got closer, the supercargo all lined the rail, looking at a line of cliffs — more like it a wall of mountains at the sea's edge. Closer in, we eventually made out a narrow, rocky gap that was for all the world like looking between the soles of a sleeping man's two feet, the big toes stuck up in the air. We ain't going in there, I though to meself, but Markab ordered the supercargo below and then took us in between the headlands, riding a rising tide with the wind on our port quarter.

The little mountains closed in around us, cliffs on either side higher than the masthead. Waves broke over rocks so close we could hear the water crash and splash. No room to maneuver. Then we was through, and the water smoothed over, the sea breeze vanished and we was in a big, salty lake. An 'I saw it all first, 'cause I was on the foredeck in charge of catting the anchor and flaking out cable so's it could be let go right quick. Ahead and on both sides were soft green hills rolling down to the water's edge. The sails flapped and hung slack as they lost the wind that had been funnelling between the cliffs. Then all of a sudden we was taken aback by a land breeze gusting down from the hills. It wasn't what you'd call a serious gybe by any account, but it took us by surprise. For a few confused moments the crew was right some busy hauling in on slack sheets and paying them out again to lee. As the staysail swung across, I flattened meself on the foredeck just in time to avoid being swept over the side. While I was horizontal, I couldn't see nothing, so like any sailor should, I got to me feet and listened for orders from the quarterdeck.

I heard, "Let go the anchor!" so I did just that, and then stepped lively as a whole lot more chain than I expected snapped across the deck and roared down the hawse-hole. The anchor grabbed bottom. Held by the bow and still driven by her sails, *Wetfoot* bucked, plunged and swivelled. In the commotion amidships, men shouted, horses screamed, their hooves drumming the deck in panic. Sails flapped overhead, something rumbled amidships, and I saw a big wet splash, enough to splatter the foot of the mizzen sail.

Wetfoot swung on her anchor, wind-rode out of the north, slow current pointing her easstward. The crew were all busy dowsing the sails as fast as they could, so there was a mess of flapping canvass between me and whatever else was going on. Still, I didn't need to be told to secure the chain now the anchor had a good hold, so that's what I was doing when big hands grabbed me shoulders and swung me around. It were two of the leading hands what had no time for me as a jumped-up sprog from another ship. They changed their grip so's both of me arms was yanked up me backbone. When I doubled over, they kicked the back of me legs. It weren't a pleasant trip astern to the quarterdeck, I can tell you, but on me way, I saw what was missing. The wagon and its load had left us.

My eager escort eased up a bit when we got to officer country astern. Abner and Markab both looked at me, real close. They didn't look happy at all, at all.

"I seen him at the wagon, looking under the tarp when I was watering the horses."

I couldn't see who it was, but by the voice it was Matt, the talkative one.

Markab shouted at me, his face so close I felt his spit.

"Who put you up to it? Who? Names! Now!" He was near to screaming. "I want to see heads going down in the wake...." He stepped back a pace, one fist coming up," ... you with them."

I got ready to get hit, 'cause held from behind as I was, there was nothing I could do to stop him. With me eyes squinched up, I almost didn't see Abner put a hand on the master's arm.

"Let him speak. I don't take him for a Fresh Starter."

Markab sucked air, bringing himself back down from his rampage. Abner took over the questioning, not so loud but real serious.

"In the name of all that's holy, why did you do it?"

I took me chances, and copied his style.

"In the name of all that's holy, why would I do such a thing? An 'why would I wait until now? I could'a led you into a bog, turned you over to the townies, pushed the wagon off the ferry, let it slip when we was hoisting it aboard, snuck up on deck at night and shoved it into the sea … but I didn't, 'cause I didn't have no reason to."

Abner's eyes were on me like to bore holes in me head. I just looked back at him. He swung his big head around to Markab.

"Do you trust your crew?" he asked.

"Every last one ... of those that I chose myself," said Markab.

I wasn't too sure if that meant me as well, and neither did Abner. Then another voice joined in from behind me.

"He's the one. He's a Fresh Starter." It was Jonas.

"So now you're all going to believe the Jonah," I said, carefully leaving out the S at the end of his name.

"Jonah!" said Markab, like he couldn't believe his ears. "Is that what he's called?"

Abner winced. He knew about Jonahs. He didn't even try explaining 'cause he knew it wouldn't work. There was a long silence during which I discovered I could stand up on me own without the help of the hands what had been holding me so tenderly. I turned me head and nodded to them to say no hard feelings, and they both gave that little half-ashamed-but-won't-admit-it look of men who know they've been over-doing it.

Markab faced Abner, teeth clenched.

"Your Jonah has scuppered our bargain."

Abner's big beard drew back a mite. I couldn't see his eyes, but Markab could, and I knew he'd seen them blink.

Suddenly, Markab was back in command of his ship and himself. Before, he had been screaming angry: now he was hard and determined. He muttered something to the officer of the watch, took a few steps to the starboard quarter, folded his arms and somehow managed to look at everyone at the same time. Abner went to him, and they talked. Argued, really. I could see the back and forth of it, even though I couldn't hear a word. Finally, Markab turned away and shouted,

"I want every last one of the supercargo off my ship, right now."

An' then we was all busy swinging out the longboats, most of the dories and even Markab's own skipper's skiff. Abner stayed on the quarterdeck, but nowhere near Markab, leaving Jonas and Matt and the other men to organize the women and children so's they'd fit into the boats. That didn't go too well, because the four of them began a whole lot of shouting and pushing and generally acting like they was the only ones with brains, which they weren't, 'cause they didn't have a ghost of a notion about what they was doin'. After a lot of stupid, useless shoving and cursin', the officer of the watch saw that they was milling about to no good purpose, and sent me forward to straighten them out, which the four of them didn't like at all, at all, the more so because the women and children all minded what I said, and went where I asked them. Wonderful what a little politeness and understanding will do, ain't it?

Pretty soon, I was in a boat, last of a flotilla muddling their way away from Wetfoot. Behind us, the crew lowered the two horses into the water so they could swim for it, the poor beasts. They made a faster and more direct job of it than most of the boats, what were overloaded with lubbers and light on men who knew what they were doing, 'cause Markab had ordered only one of his men to each of the boats. After a lot of splashing about, they settled down and began to row up the bay and around what turned out to be a little island. Eventually, we landed them all at a pebble beach below a tall, grassy dyke with a zig-zag path up to the top, maybe six or eight times a man's height. I could have been across the water and up a tree in the time it took the rest of them to make it, but...

Hold on now. I'm getting ahead of meself.

Go back to the middle of the bay, me with a port oar, Abner to starboard, side by each on the same thwart. He'd been last to leave, of course. I'd lost sight of him in the kerfuffle of boarding until he appeared beside me while I was seeing the last of the men, women and children into the final boat, which I was set to row all on me own. I was shoving off from Wetfoot's salt-stained port side, when Abner climbed down the scrambling net and stepped aboard beside me like he did it every day. He was handy, or experienced, or both, because we fell into an easy rhythm that moved the boat along on a steady course -- something that couldn't be said for most of the other craft splashing, yawing and swerving into each other astern of us.

"So," said Abner, measuring out his words between pulls on his oar, "How long ago was it when you ran away to sea?"

"Near on five years. How ...?"

"Did I guess? You're smarter than the other, older sailors."

"Who says?"

"I do. They do. You do every time you open your mouth. You're educated."

"Not enough to make me an officer."

"Enough to read, write and cypher, I'm betting. More important, you think, and you can do it under pressure. You're worth promoting."

"That's happened. Here aboard *Wetfoot.*"

"And will it be as promised aboard *Stella*?"

"How'd you know…"

"I'm a good listener."

"Leading hand, wage and share, when I get back to me ship."

"Is that good enough?"

"For now."

"Are you sure it'll all happen the way they said?"

That shut me mouth. I kept busy pulling at me oar and checking over me shoulder at where we were heading, and then looking astern to see how the other boats were doing, all the while remembering how Markab had been ready to cut and run, leaving the supercargo to fend for themselves. That had me wondering whether Nair would honour the masters' promise, or whether all they'd offered had been only bait to dangle in front of a foolish fish -- me.

Just beyond me feet, sitting on the stern thwart were four of the youngsters. They were more than children and less than grown up, and hurt bad by all that they had gone through. The two boys 'faces were sullen, brooding. The two girls 'eyes looked down. They all sat silent, in pain from the past, and in fear of the future. I remembered one of Al's sayings: "Unhappy are those who know the worst too young."

Then, like he'd been thinking me thoughts, Abner spoke to the women and children around us in the boat, who were keeping still with the patience of the hopeless. I don't remember his words, but they worked a charm on the mums and their little ones -- and the older ones, too. They all looked at him the way children watch the eyes of someone telling them a story, and they was comforted. Some of the boys began to look around with something close to curiosity, and the eyes of the two girls got into focus.

As we swung forward to begin a stroke of the oars, Abner's head was close to mine.

"Sophie and Imogene are looking you over," he whispered.

I concentrated on rowing. Two strokes later he whispered again.

"Could be your share if you joined."

That was too much too soon, said one corner of me mind. But the rest of me imagination started telling me stories about a life ashore with a young wife. One of the girls smiled shyly at me, and I felt meself blush.

"Who deep sixed the guns?" I asked, to change the subject.

"Wasn't me or mine behind the … (stroke) … accident," he grunted, almost missing his stroke. "But whoever it was cost me a bundle times three."

"How so?"

"Bought them. (stroke) Bought horses and wagon to drag them north. (stroke) Promised most to Markab as passage-money. (stroke) He called the loss a deal-breaker. (stroke) Had to pay him gold to land us here. (stroke) No leverage. (stroke) No protection. (stroke) Not a good beginning for The Fort."

"The Fort?"

"Where we're headed. Where you could be welcomed. (stroke) Needed."

The last word came out between his clenched teeth, and was almost lost in his beard, but I heard him, and I glowed. Abner valued me, and that was a whole lot more than how I'd been treated by Markab. Abner's approval meant more than the girls, even more than adventure. And he had reason, I told myself. I'd saved him and his family, worked with him to bring the lot of them aboard, helped them through the voyage, got them into the boats.… Of course I was valuable to him. Much more than I was to Markab, that flint-hearted schemer who'd gouged money out of Abner. He'd been ready to abandon the lot of them. Besides, what did Markab need guns for, anyway?

I rowed on, while a story spun out in me head. A real satisfying tale about how Abner made me his right-hand man, his counsellor, his friend, his lost boy what had gotten himself found again, just like the yarn about the prodigal son.

And then when I looked up, one of the two girls looked at me kind of sideways, they way women do like it's a question that you're supposed to know the answer to, and then they looked at each other, and giggled.

I felt me face go hot again, so I concentrated on rowing. Part of me was lost in that story about a new life ashore with a wife and a valued position in a better place than I'd ever imagined possible.

Then Abner nudged me with his shoulder because we'd overtaken all the other boats and were almost at the pebble beach. We swung our boat around to land stern first, so's it would be easier for getting the women and children ashore. Abner jumped out to wave at the other boats, leaving me to make sure nobody fell in, which fitted right into the story in me head. There I was, all full of meself, taking the hands of the mums, like I was a part of something real important, passing the littlies to their sisters, and helping the girls ashore with both of me hands around their middles, ho, ho, ho; and having the time of me life.

And then I made a grab for the last girl in the boat. She was standing on a thwart with her back to me and a littlie on her hip, both of them like to topple into the water, but she slapped me hands away and jumped ashore on her own, littlie and all. Then she tipped up her face what had been hidden in a scarf, and I saw it was the skinny girl, confusin'ly named Michael, holding her little sister, Sally.

"Stupid sailor!" said Sally happily in her little-girl's voice.

So there I was with me mouth hanging open and nothing coming out of it, looking at the pair of them. Sally stuck her thumb in her mouth and waved her fat little fingers in a bye-bye, but Michael didn't even turn around as she headed up the zig-zag path along with the folk from the other boats.

"There's gratitude," said Abner. "However, if you look up and a bit to your right, you'll see Sophie and Imogene."

Well, they was a sailor's dream and no mistake. Two girls, just turned women in all the right places, looking at me like I was the last biscuit on the plate.

"You don't have to choose," said Abner. "Unless, of course, two is too much for you."

Once more, me mouth hung open and nothing came out. I suppose I had just assumed that there were more men ashore, waiting for the wives Abner was bringing them.

You're probably wondering how anyone could have missed it, but until that moment, standing with me feet in the water, hanging on to the longboat, it never even crossed me simple mind that Abner and the men with him were the only roosters in a sizeable hen-house, and what's more, he was offering me a two-girl share.

So you see, me mind wasn't working at its usual high level of accomplishment. I was young, and caught between wind and water, wanting and wishing with an itchy feeling in the back of me head that all this weren't right.

It took me a while to realize I was being shouted at.

"Angel! You deaf as well as stupid? Get your boat out of the way!"

It was the first mate. Five years of taking orders, and you do what you're told without argument. I clambered aboard me longboat, pulled it out into the stream and leaned on me oars, looking at the boats getting tangled up as they all tried to find room to unload. It were a mess. Most of the women were unsteady, what with their skirts and their bags and baggages getting in their way, to say nothing about the boys who were bumping into everything and each other as they all tried to be first. Abner and his men were shouting, and so were the sailors. A couple of the younger boys fell into the shallows and had to be fished out, dripping wet and scared. Just about everybody got wet to the knees and beyond.

And as I sat there, leaning on me oars, I was drifting away from the beach and I was also drifting away from the stories I'd been telling meself about the life I could have ashore. The two girls who fancied me were lost in the crowd, what was now mostly out of the boats and straggling up the. steep, zig-zag path to whatever waited for them beyond. A part of me wanted to go back and help Abner sort it all out, the way we'd worked together aboard the ferry, but the current was taking me out into the bay, and one by one the other boats were getting rid of their passengers and turning seaward, and top of that, well, the habit of being a sailor took hold, and I started the long pull back to the ship. On the way, words came to me that I could have said to Michael, none of them right, all of them too late. All I had to remember was the back of her head and, over her shoulder, little Sally waving bye-bye..

Seven

Well, now you know about me beginnings, and why Abner got started messing about with other people's lives. There's more to be said about that, but you ain't ready for it yet, 'cause at the time, neither was I.

Y'know, when yer start looking back on yer life, you notice times when everything might'a gone in a whole different direction. Supposing it had been that I waded ashore, followed Abner, and got accepted into what he called his family. Would things have been different? For certain sure, it would have made my life over from the ground up, but it might well have ground me down, too.

Still and all, a lot hung on what I decided -- that's not the right word. I should say, from what happened, 'cause I didn't decide. I drifted on me oars, and took orders from Markab, a man who had even less use for me than I had for him, instead of taking an offer from Abner, who I might' a helped. But then, I might'a made things worse, although that's hard to believe.

I got back aboard *Wetfoot*, and as we sailed south and away from Abner's fort, I took to wondering about what I'd missed. Strangely, I wasn't remembering those two girls what had looked at me like they'd be all kinds of willin'. It was Sally's giggles I heard in me mind, and Michael's copper-coloured hair that I saw. An' me eyes went all funny, like from looking too long at the horizon.

I couldn't say why.

Once I was back aboard, it were like icicles had grown on everything, starting with Markab. He took one look at me, never said a word, but it were clear that he blamed me for his fee being on the bottom, like he had shouted it for everyone to hear. He never said one word, because he knew it weren't so, but that meant he hated me all the more. His feeling spread to everyone.

So that's maybe part of why I didn't make me mark aboard *Wetfoot*, although it's for certain sure I'd have had to be the incarnation of all that's seamanlike to have gained any approval from Enif and his mates. The one thing on which we were agreed was that me going back to *Stella* couldn't happen too soon.

A couple of unpleasant weeks later, we was at sea, no land in sight, when the lookout yelled "Sail Ho!"

I was on deck, keeping the green hands busy at the never-ending business of make and mend what keeps a ship goin, 'and getting no thanks for it, when I heard Markab telling Enif to swing out a longboat and get ready to pull over to *Stella*.

Back then, I had no idea how the master had done it. It seemed to me like luck or fate or magic that two ships could arrive at the same place in the middle of nothing but ocean in all directions. But I didn't have much time to stand about wondering, 'cause Enif told me to grab me kit and stand ready to leave. First time I ever saw him smile, and it weren't what yer call heartwarming. By the time I had me bag at me feet, waiting by the longboat, *Wetfoot* was hove to about a cable's length from *Stella*, what had done the same.

When we'd rowed over and come alongside, Markab went up the scrambling net. Enif waved me up behind him. He and the boat's crew just hung on and waited. When I came over the rail, Markab and Nair were together on the quarterdeck, their heads close, Markab sharing the bad news, for sure.

After days of feeling invisible aboard *Wetfoot*, I was glad to see me mates aboard *Stella*. Not that we were close, mind, but we'd known each other long enough to be comfortable. I'd had the wit to put me nice blue jacket in the bottom of me dunnage, so I fit right back in without nobody thinking I was giving meself airs. In a few days, it were like I'd never been away. Some people asked me what life aboard *Wetfoot* was like, so I told them what they wanted to hear -- that it weren't a patch on *Stella* and her crew.

I should have been all nice and comfy in me old bunk and doing the jobs I knew with me mates, but something had changed aboard while I was *Wetfoot*, and I couldn't get me head around what it was. Something in the wind, you might say, but it was lost on me at the time.

To make a whole bunch of short stories even shorter, I'll just say that I sailed on *Stella* to a considerable number of ports of call up and down the coast to the north of the expanding disaster area what had been the towns and cities destroyed by the Rot and the Fresh Starters. I had good times with happy meetings ashore and enough desperate moments afloat to make me a pile of remembrances, some fine, some that I ain't all that proud of. But more than sometimes I wondered what might'a happened to Michael and little Sally.

What helped was making port from time to time. Decent-sized towns, too, maybe three or four times the size of where I'd been born. I liked the look of the buildings, many of them right tall, maybe four or five stories high, even if some of them were chewed-looking, like something had bitten them off for growing to high, the way a man will whack the tops off flowers with a stick. You'd think that every port would be different, and so they were from the shape of the harbours to the layout of the towns, but the people were pretty much the same as you'll find anywhere: a mixture of all different sizes, shapes and shades. There were fishermen, sailors and men who work the docks, most of them too busy with their own lives to do more than nod at you if you caught their eye over a beer-mug in a tavern. Then there were the ones with soft hands, wearing clothes that never felt a capful of seawater hit them, nor a sack of flour on the shoulder, neither. Just about all of them were full-of-themselves and bossy, with no time for an ordinary seaman, that's for sure.

And then there was the women and girls. Like usual, there was the ones what seemed real outgoing and friendly, but with a hand in your pocket, like as not. Those were the ones old Al had warned me against, and I heeded him 'cause whatever he said old Holy wanted, what scared me off was the diseases he told me I could catch. So I stuck to looking, and I looked real careful. There was the women doing jobs like working behind the counters in ships' chandlers, slinging mugs of ale in taverns or buying and sellin'. I liked what I saw, 'cause they mostly didn't give themselves airs. These were the fishermen's, shopkeepers 'and merchants 'wives, the ones what had no time or inclination for the companionship of anyone but their shore-staying man, and good luck to them .

Now so far, I'm talking about the people you'd meet if yer never walked any further away from the dock than you could get in a couple dozen strides. But if you get back a piece from the salt water, you find the town that's holding its skirts up to the ankles like an old lady on a muddy road. Back where the nice folks live, away from the common stuff that goes on near the water, there's what you call society, what was a long up-wind beat from me own world of making do with what you've got.

I discovered a long way back when I was still a wharf-rat running errands that the grown-up mucky-mucks in them big mansions, as well as them what's in the smaller and more envious envious houses, all have precious little time for the fishermen what bring them the fish they eat or the sailors what brings them the good stuff across the water from away. But that ain't true of their young ones, not at all, at all. The boys wonder about being bad and running away to sea. The girls wonder about how bad the bad boys really are.

Right. Here's what I figgered. There had to be more'n one of them wondering girls what wanted to know more about the boys from down there at the water's edge and beyond, where their mums won't let them go, but they also want those boys to be good looking. Which I was. And clean, which I could be soon as I got to fresh water. And well-spoken, what I could do too, thanks to Al. And bad, which is what I figgered they would see in me eyes. An' I cunningly decided that it didn't hurt me chances none to wear a nice blue almost-new jacket and a hat, not like the common sailors at all at all. So thinking of meself as some great romancer, I imagined sneaking around the edges of society ashore, exchanging glances, now and then, stealing a kiss, maybe more. Remembering the respect old Al had taught me, I decided never to tell lies, although I admit that me overall plan were economical with the truth and right tight-lipped where promises were concerned.

Mind you, that owed more to the way me Da behaved than to anything old Al had said. Growing up, watching how me Da talked to the women in his life I'd come to the conclusion that a sailor's promise ain't worth much, special when he's ashore and telling a girl that there's just one more voyage and he'll never leave her again.

Time's like those, a man's pulled two ways -- seawards and shorewards -- between what he is and what she is. 'Cause she's the other part of being alive what you don't have with you when you're voyaging on the briny. And when you find her ashore, it's no matter if she's younger or older, blonder or darker, shorter or taller, she's what you've almost forgotten you were looking for, and were just holding as an empty space, ready and waiting, sort of like you hope she'll be waiting for you, which she is, except she's not the same woman every time, except of course, that she is, cause she ain't a woman, she's woman.

And woman is what men think they need when their ship makes landfall, when the coastline shows up ahead and it's where they were heading all the time, holding back the skip-a-heartbeat moment of fearing that you're lost somewhere between sea and sky with only the prospect of taking that last desperate breath when it's going to be water you're breathing next, which everyone knows full well you can't. Don't think I didn't feel it, but you gotta remember that Al brought me up on a some heavy diet of warnings about the evil of fornication, the depravity of whoring, and if that weren't persuasive enough, all the real and nasty diseases a young man could acquire from the smiling purveyors of untold delight.

At sea, I kept on wanting and hoping and scheming. Ashore, after I'd washed me face and hands, shifted into me neat blue jacket and hat, and set me plan into operation I found out that I hadn't reckoned with the girls' da's and ma's and brothers, uncles and aunties, too. Them desirable girls were so well hedged and walled and circled and protected that I soon was heading back to me ship with me topsails set for fair, and no wind in them . Truth to tell, all of me shore leaves ended with me on the wharf waiting for the longboat with nothing but lies to swap with me mates.

I'm running on again. An' yer laughing at me, lass. I can see it in your eyes. An' you too, lad. Well, go ahead. Have yer chuckle at me foolish youth.

Are y' done yet? I got more to tell yer.

So now we're talking over a year and a bit after I left Abner's Fort. By then, I had done more than me five years aboard *Stella*. It was thenabouts there was this evil moment I have to tell you, 'cause it's part of me story, and not just an old man rambling on about happier days.

Stella was a good ship, and had been lucky mainly because Nair kept us safe from the shore sickness, choosing his ports of call, and restricting shore leave when he had to go where things weren't all that good. Some of the men wanted to chance it so's they could have their fun with the sailors 'friends, but they all stopped their grumbles the day we were hailed by a little schooner almost out of sight from the harbour we was heading for.

Nair took us close enough that we could see the crew, and it weren't pretty. As we came up to loo'ard of them, I caught a whiff of something rotten, and it weren't fish, it was the men aboard -- and women too. There were some laying on the deck who had to be dead, or near it. The ones who tried to speak us were so next to gone they weren't making no sense -- just a god-awful weak wailing and screaming from voices what weren't working no more. Hard to believe they were alive, they were so covered in scars and open sores and ….

Even now, I don't like to think about it, because we left them to die. Small comfort it was and is that they'd probably done the same to folks ashore.

Nair had us haul up a half-empty keg of fresh water and float it downwind to them, along with a sack of biscuit in a bucket -- as if that could make it right. We did it, though we all knew it weren't doing no good.

The very next day Nair called the ship's company together and gave us the news that we were going to what he called the City of the Sea, where we'd be meeting up with our sister-ships. He named them off, along with their masters, which by now meant something to me, particularly *Silver Swan*, better known in the fo'c's'le as the *Dirty Duck*, on which I'd seen them two brown eyes what I'd never had the chance to know better. You remember I told you about her, back a piece. Well, I was turning over the memory of them eyes, and feeling right some curious about me prospects, so to speak, that I hardly heard the master rambling on about "transfers, promotions and discharges."

So, sure as sin and suffering, the very next day we saw ships on the horizon, right where we were heading. As we got closer, there were us and nine more three-masted schooners dowsing their sails and rafting together. I never saw nothing like it in me life, and don't expect to see it again, either. Close your eyes and think up a ragged island made of ten hulls with a forest of masts above them, some of them raked, some standing straight up and tall, most of them gaff-rigged on all masts, two or three with yards crossed for a square tops'l ahead, two of them staysail rigged — all of them furling their sails to lie together with a gentle wind taking them nowhere in particular. If you'd been there with me, you'd have been amazed at the masters ' seamanship as they took their ships in closer and closer until heaving lines flew from deck to deck and we all scurried about deploying the fenders and spinning the spiderweb that held us side by each so's we could set the gangways and link ship to ship.

When the fleet had got itself sorted, *Stella* lay to starboard of *Cygnus*, with *Tidewalker, Eclipse* and *Seachild* to port, and then *Silver Swan, Spindrift* and *Whisper*, their great hulls gently rising and falling like they were folk sleeping together in a bed. Last to arrive was *Elusive* on the outside edge, with a little ketch in tow dangling off her stern like a puppy on a string.

As you can imagine, masters and their senior officers were first across the gangways, heading for *Cygnus*, the number one ship. Since we were next door, so to speak, I got a good look at most of them meeting and greeting the man I knew from scuttlebutt was the Grand Master of the lot of them there at The City of the Sea.

He was tall, and he stood tall, if y'know what I mean. No mistaking who was in charge, even without him being the only one wearing a black cloak from his shoulders to his boot heels. I knew right away that this was Zubin. Fact is, I heard his name the first day I came aboard *Stella*, but I paid it no mind at the time. Then over the years I suppose you could say that the name and the man who owned it soaked into me mind until I could tell the stories I'd heard about him to the boys and men who had joined the ship after me.

Zubin were a legend. Masters, officers and men all believed that Zubin led his men fair but firm, and if he provisioned and outfitted his ship to be the envy of the fleet, then he only did so to make the others want to do better. And then there were great tales about how he'd chased punished pirates, how he caught a sea-monster, or the time he took down a mutineer without laying a hand on him. Most of all, there were the yarns about how he had out-sailed every ship that tried to get the better of him.

You can guess that I was right pleased to watch him meet the masters and their officers on his quarterdeck. Seeing the way they all respected Zubin made me consider the transfers, promotions and discharges that Nair had been going on about, which I'd ignored until that moment, because for a while the idea of discharges was top of me mind. I'd not been all that keen to sign on for another five years, since there'd been no more talk of promotions since Markab had put me back aboard *Stella*, first taking care to poison Nair's mind about me, so that the venom dripped down through the officers even to me shipmates, making them more'n a little distant and suspicious. I was wondering whether I could be looking at being transferred to a new ship with a promotion to ease the strain.

So there I was, looking at the other nine ships all obedient to their summoning at the City of the Sea, thinking that Zubin might work the magic to give me the right to wear the blue officer's jacket in me kitbag that Markab had bought me so's Abner would figger I could be trusted. The stories about Zubin that I'd heard and re-told had worked me over, you see, making me into a believer that the man was a holy living angel, the shining light of righteous leadership for all seagoing men, a master what could look into hearts and souls of his men and do justice for the oppressed. Come to think of it, that was the kind of language I'd used to re-tell the Zubin stories to the new recruits. At the time, I'd thought I was just spinning the good yarns I'd heard, but as I kept doing it, I talked myself into believing what I'd wished and wanted to be true, because if it were true, then everything would all make sense -- the work, the orders, the way masters and their officers rule the lives of their crews. And laying aside all that bilge about how things are supposed to work but don't, after going on six years, I was hoping for a fair share in the shape of a promotion.

Standing there in the waist of *Stella*, looking up at the masters on *Cygnus* 'quarterdeck, I had hopes. But that didn't last too bleeding long, I can tell you. That night, I tried to find the girl aboard *Silver Swan*, the one with the eyes. No luck. She'd found herself a big, good-looking feller in one of them blue officers' jackets. So I made do with a few too many mugs of what the hands were calling "City beer" -- a special brew with a serious kick to it. I spent the best part of the night getting lubricated, feeling sorry for meself. An 'that led to me remembering how it felt to be respected by Abner. Confusing me even more were thoughts about the two girls he'd tempted me with. And while looking into me severalth mug, I found meself thinking of the skinny girl I'd first seen ashore on that midnight march so long ago.

Next morning Nair called all hands on deck, and far too early, by me way of thinking. I slid into a bit of shade alongside the mizzenmast and squinted into more light than I'd wanted or asked for. Then the whole crew started banging their heels on the deck in honour of Zubin, who came across the gangway, looking real impressive all in black, with his cloak hanging off his shoulders down his back right to the deck. Nair's fist came up to his throat in a full salute as the heeling ended, and he handed Zubin the muster roll -- the book listing every last one of our names, who we were and what Nair thought of us.

They started with the officers. Nair read out the names, and Zubin did the honours. And so they worked their way down the list of promotions, confirmations, and commendations. I stood there, blinking at them, wondering when me name would come up. Like Al used to say, "Hope springs eternal." I listened as the pair of them worked their way through the names of the leading hands, able, ordinary and on down to boy seamen, with never a mention of Able Angel.

I was still holding me breath, when Nair read a name I didn't know and Zubin spoke what they call words of farewell to some poor soul what had been deep sixed before I came aboard. Then on they droned, ending up with good old Smitty, who was the last man in the sad list of poor souls who had fed the fishes. The only cold comfort for a man with a hangover who had done everything he was asked and ordered to do, and then a bit more, was that I wasn't dead.

And then they put me and a handful of other poor sods from around the fleet onto that little ketch, cut us adrift and sailed over the horizon.

Best I pack it in for now. I don't want to talk about that day ever again.

.

Eight

You're back, I see, and expecting me to go on with me story, no doubt. Well, yer out of luck, 'cause I don't remember what happened next.

What I've been telling you so far is clear like a picture in me head, all in colour, with the wind on me cheek and the sails sighing overhead, and the promise of a mug-up with mates with yarns to spin when the watch is over. Speaking of which …

Fine, I don't mind if I do. An' good on you for bringing it, lass.

Well, now, you want me to go on. And I would, except that the next two times ten years of me life and more are lost in me wake like rope ends what gets tossed over the side, never to be seen again. If I try to salvage what's lost, I get a hank of this and a short-end of that, and they all fall apart when I try to wind them into a yarn that makes any sense.

What I'm trying to say is that the next twenty or so years happened, and now they're lost like the memory of whatever I ate a week ago. I know there were good and bad times, same way as I know I must have ate something, but I only know that for sure 'cause I'm still here, ain't I?

Thanks for the re-fill, lass.

Somewhere or somewhen a long time later, I woke up to the fact that of all the men and boys from all the ships at the City of the Sea what got dumped mid-ocean with not even a compass, I was the only one left. Some jumped ship at the first port, what we got to by the simple process of heading into the sunset and asking the folks ashore where we'd got to. That were me own idea, and what 'stablished me as a man what could keep his head on straight when everyone else was panicked witless, as surely they were. When we had land within spitting distance and knew where we were at, we said good riddance to the ones who said they'd never set foot in a ship ever again.

And so those of us what had no business with or wish to remain ashore began our new life, sailing up and down the coast, fishin', tradin', sometimes thievin', and occasionally picking up new crew to replace the ones what got fed up with the seafaring life. And a strange and wonnerful bunch they were. Not one of them could make sense of a chart, open a book — still less read the rutter what was me own personal and private log of where we went, who did what, how much it made, and why. It weren't what you call an edifying moral story, but now I look back, I wish I still had it — or rather, them, 'cause by the time twenty and more years had vanished in me wake there was more'n a few well-thumbed books in me locker, all of them filled up with courses to steer, rocks, reefs and shoals to beware of, and the names of those precious few folk what could be trusted — and a lot more. Getting it down on paper is good for you, I discovered, even if it's only a scribble of notes on what the weather was doing that day.

Who was I with? Without me rutters,

I don't even recall names, I wrote them all down and then forgot them. Who was we? Rejects. At first, we was the dozen who, like me, weren't judged good enough to become Men of the Sea. Later, me shipmates were rejects from whatever they'd done ashore, which were a monster pile of unwanted this and unsavoury that.

Most of what we did you can call tradin': buying cheap and selling dear. Making do. Staying alive, which meant keeping a long way away from the remains of ports and towns and cities that used to be the hearts and arteries of trade until they turned into depraved, festering, plague-ridden cess-pools where lived what once had been human.

"Woe unto ye," is what old Habakuk said to the sinners in his tribe, but he wouldn't have wasted words on them that was still alive in them cities. They was beyond all hope of redemption.You don't do repent-and-return-to-holiness numbers on folks who are trying to bite you in the neck so's you'll be infected like they are, and live out your really short life doing depravity with them, to spite everything you once believed.

Sometimes when we were passing downwind, we thought we could smell the Rot. Be that as it may, for certain sure we could see the black smoke rising from where people who once went about their daily lives, just getting on with life, not thinking about what might be happening someplace else, figgering that bad stuff happened to other people, until it happened to them, and it was too late to do nothing but die.

As the years went by, the smokes got fewer and farther between. A dozen years, and where whole cities had smouldered like one great big trash-fire, there was clear air and a fresh breeze, and the only smokes were the thin wisps rising from campfires lit by scavengers.

Never went there, meself. But we traded with men — and women, too — what did. Middle-men is what they were, scary folks what risked the Rot to gather whatever looked valuable. Then there was us, cautiously getting and expensively selling to the lucky ones what lived in ports and towns that the plagues and the craziness had missed — usually because they'd cut themselves off back when it all went wrong. Risky business it was for us, but profitable. We ate well, drank more'n we should have, and we each salted away our unfair share of gold, silver, and valuable goods, all of our treasures hidden somewhere every one of us never told the others.

At the time, I could remember faces and places and names, but they're all blurred to nothing now. Some of me crew were only around for a few months, until they'd got what they thought was enough to start afresh ashore. Some were only aboard from one port to the next, where some sailor's friend no doubt relieved them of whatever coin they had with them. I was the one that lasted. A handful hung on with me. Over the years, the names changed, but by and large, me crew were pretty much the same. We were men who had learned how to stand well clear of each others' vices, the nicest of which was drink and women ashore. An' about the rest, the least said the better.

A few years after we was let slip from the fleet, when I had become the only one aboard who had served with the Men of the Sea, I began to think of the ketch as mine, and 'cause of that, the men who came aboard saw me as the one what decided. I kept it loose — never asked to be called master or even skipper. Eventually, they all did that out of habit, 'cause I was the one what hollered, "Ready about!' or "Reef the main, you bastards!" Or, "First thing, we get watered, provisioned, and replace that dodgy storm jib. Then we hit the pubs. Right?"

And they took it from me, and did like I told them, and when they got to arguing they even quieted down and let me sort things out before knives got drawn and blood spilt. Mark you, me methods weren't all kindness and sweet reason: sometimes I had to take action by scragging some rotter before he got the drop on me. Anyway, like I said, the ketch became mine. Mine to lead, mine to care for, mine to keep shipshape. An' I took pride in her.

Efficient is what we was, the ones with staying power, that is. We got good at what we did, although there was little good in it. I was handy before it started, 'cause I'd learned well from Smitty, and I'd went on learning after he was gone. Then going on for a quarter of a century I kept on getting better, building up experience, learning from it, recognizing the signs. Like knowing when to make sail and when to reef — if you can stretch that idea to take in a whole lot more than seamanship.

We saved each other's lives when it was in our interest to do so. We could have let stupidity take its due, as we had seen so often happen, but we needed the unsaid but binding bargain, "I saved your skin, now you owe me." Sometimes what we had to pay in return were right ugly, but we couldn't say no, because sooner or later we'd need a favour in return. It all worked because we all believed in some kind of a balance, a give and take that evened out — even though all the evidence was that it didn't.

You know what was the worst of it? No friends. No real shipmates. Each one of us was dealing for himself, thinking he'd win a bigger pile than the others. All of us fearing we'd be the next to get left behind — as we'd done a few times when someone got too much to live with.

Those times were all grey. Grey at sea, grey ashore, where I went only 'cause I had to. No joy in them.

What? No, I think not, thank'ee. I still have a couple of swigs left in me mug, and when they're done, I'll have a little snooze. Maybe see you tomorrow? Perhaps. If I'm lucky — and you're not.

Nine

Oh all right, there is more what I hinted at when I begun this yarnin'. It began when colour got to seeping back in around the edges of me life. Not like them grey years I don't have the will or the wish to remember.

It started in some port south of here, but then pretty much everything is, right? My plan was to careen the ketch and scrape her bottom. First, we put in to a little town — not much more than a village — to replenish the eatables, pick up drinkables and see what the folks thereabouts were like. Looking back, that was me own mistake. I should'a scraped first, and partied ashore after, but at the time I thought we needed beer to help us through the hot and sweaty business of peeling the weed and barnacles off the hull. Anyway, after a couple days of shore leave, most of which I spent in a nice little pub eating shore food what somebody else had cooked, and gamming with the local fishermen, we slipped our lines and headed off to the almost next door cove, what I'd learned about in the pub.

We headed up a river what emptied out a couple miles east of an abandoned village where once there had been a little settlement of folk what eventually either died off or decided it was safer to live where they weren't out on their lonesomes. We rowed and hauled the ketch far enough upstream so's the fresh water would do some of our work for us by loosening up what she'd grown on her bottom at sea. Nice quiet place it was. Swift water below a little falls chuckling to itself, and a convenient spur of rock to serve as a mooring. Mixed forest on both sides, and a sand beach a stone's throw away to port.

When I was up in the bow, checking the set of the shore-line for the night, I heard me crew below whispering and laughing about sleeping ashore where I wouldn't be rousing them early, so when they told me they wanted to light a fire on the beach just for the hell of it, I believed them, and sacked out for the night aboard, leaving them to the beer they'd brought and the mosquitos they hadn't counted on.

Next morning, they was gone. I sat down in the cockpit, lit me pipe and looked at where they'd been. Right behind the remains of their fire, I saw the beginnings of a little path that looked like it ran through the forest to the village where I'd stayed too long. That got me started figgering what to do if the mean spirited buggers was up to something evil. I suspicioned they weren't planning anything good, but if it was only taking another day before we careened and scraped, I didn't want to be too hasty, because it could be they'd just gone for more beer. Still, I decided it would be a good day to clean me rifle and check the ammunition.

I s'pose I should tell you that I'd gotten over me horror of guns after more than two decades of meeting people ashore what already had them. If nobody has guns, nobody needs them, but if some do, everyone does — at least that was what I thought back then.

Anyway, I was thinking things over in the morning sunshine, oiling and loading me rifle, listening to the hush of the falls and the gurgle of the stream under the counter when this young fellow came out of the woods onto the beach. He was about me own height, carrot-red hair, strong but scrawny, like he was fit but wasn't getting enough to eat. He wore yer basic faded-to-no-colour canvas breeks and a black tarpaulin jacket, cut loose and large, hanging around him, spite of the fact it were a pleasant summer's day. He took one look behind him, listening, took another look at the ketch, didn't see me, and headed for the dory, what me crew had used to go ashore. It seemed to me that he had a mind to steal me ship.

"You get away from the dory," I told him, and stood up. "I got me a gun, and yer an easy shot from here."

He froze, looking at me, calculating the odds.

"I'll take me chances. I'm dead anyway if they catch me."

Well, that got me curious. Still, I took out me rifle and made a show out of loading it. He saw, but it didn't stop him. He got himself over the t'other side of the dory, crouched down low as he could, and started shoving it into the water. Trouble was, it were a full-size, heavy old thing, and me rotten shipmates had run it up the shore, the bleeders. The lad would get his back up aging it, shove until his feet dug in, and move the thing mebby a hand span. But he kept on tryin', and that took me fancy, too.

"Who's after you, and why?" I asked, resting the rifle on the cabin-top, and sighting down the barrel at him.

"Shopkeeper ..." he says, and gives a grunt as he moved the dory another hand span. "Claimed I stole from his till."

"An' did you?" I asked.

"Nope. It were the sailors that came from — here, I guess. They're after me now."

Right about then, we both heard three or four voices I knew, all telling each other what to do next, the way folk do when there ain't nobody in charge. The lad gave one last desperate shove, the dory broke free and slid into the stream, and if he hadn't hung on, he'd have lost it. He scrambled aboard, wet to the knees. It were then he notices he ain't got no oars. Me shipmates, the cunning bastards, had hid them in the woods, out of which come me four scruffy-looking crew, all out of puff from running.

"Stop 'im! Grab 'im! Shoot 'im!" they yells at me.

"An' why should I be doing yer dirty work?" said I, and like an idiot, stood up to talk.

Which was when I saw one of them pull out a little pistol and take aim at me. Now nobody can hit much with a short-barrel pocket gun 'lest they're just about on top of whoever they're shooting at, and least of all if they've been running. Still, being aimed at brings a feller up short and some bright awake, let me tell yer. Before he could bang off his first shot, I was on me knees with a good thick oaken cockpit coaming atween him and me. Damn fool went on firing; twice, right quick. I was breathing fast, and thinking faster, putting together what I'd been too thick to take notice of. Sure enough, the shooter were the one I'd heard leading the whispering the evening before, and now it looked like he'd been persuasive with his mates. While they were ashore, the double-dealing, treacherous bastards had probably chased after the youngster, so's they'd have someone to blame when they grabbed the ketch off me and sailed away, leaving me and the lad to feed the fishes.

Well, being too late at guessing their plan made me a mite testy, so I stayed hunkered down behind the cockpit coaming and the cabin, then chose me moment and stuck up me rifle and blew the first of them off his feet. I must've only clipped his jacket, 'cause he were up on one knee and shooting again before I could reload. His mates left him where he was and ran back into the cover of the woods, where they started shooting at me as well.

Now here I should explain to the pair of you that this weren't the first time me and the ketch had been threatened by pirates, attacked by thieves, stalked and shot at by unfriendly folk. On account of what you   call that prior educational experience, I seldom dropped me valuable cast iron anchor when I could make do with a killick or a line to shore. That way, I always had the option of doing a sneaky slip and run. Experience also having taught me not to make a target of meself on the foredeck, I pulled the end of the slippery hitch what I'd rigged up the night before, spun the wheel, and off I went downstream after the dory, with nasty little splashes in the water to starboard where the silly buggers were still banging away with their piddly little pistols.

It was then, when there was no going back, that it came to me that sailing the ketch alone meant I'd be making and tending sail, and standing all watches, which is more than one man can keep on doing beyond a day or so. Howsomever, it was for certain sure that I had no wish to see me mutinous crew ever again. Then it occurred to me that right there floating downstream ahead of me were a likely young lad who just might make me another pair of hands till I could recruit more and better. So I unrolled the jib, caught enough of a breeze to get steerage way, overhauled the dory as it swung around a little bend in the stream where the fresh met the salt-chuck, and brung the young fellow aboard.

Soon he were going, "Ah ... thanks, I guess," as he stood dripping onto the cockpit sole, and looking at me real cautious-like, "An' just in time. That dory was taking me out to sea."

"So, where would you be wanting t'go, young feller?" I asks him.

"Home."

"An' where might that be?"

"North. A long way north of here."

It being a fair bet that me scummy ex-shipmates what was willing to shoot me to get the ketch wouldn't be expecting me to sail north alone, so I nodded, stuck out me hand and said:

"Well, then, that's where we'll go."

He took me hand, rolled up his tarpaulin jacket and tossed it down the companionway, where it landed with a hard and heavy thump that at the time I didn't think to question, 'cause when he was peeling off, I was admiring the good quality cream-coloured shirt he wore underneath.

And that's how I began me voyage back to where Markab landed Abner and his motley crew of too few men, too many women, and a skinny little girl with a fat little sister, both of whom what had no use for me.

Did'ja bring beer? Good.

Ten

Turned out, where the lad wanted to go was a damn sight further than the two-three days' sailing what I'd 'magined.' Course, I didn't know at the time where we'd end up, cause I was thinking me new crew came from one of them little fishing villages along the coast.

We worked our way north for a week or more, past a couple ports and harbours I'd visited before, and a few I hadn't, till we were beyond the latitude where I'd always turned back south again. Not because I didn't have a hankering to see what came next, but because me previous shipmates would have none of going where the compass pointed every which way but north, and what's more, did it while you watched it spin. Which is something that don't inspire confidence when yer blind in fog and don't know how far y'are from land.

We'd left a gunk-hole bay where we'd spent the night, and I was expecting the lad — did I say he called hisself Jim? — to say, "Far enough, take me to the next village just ahead," but instead he says, all cool and collected, "With this nor'west wind and a clear enough sky for the stars to keep us on course, we can raise the coast around Charton when the sun comes up, or real soon after."

Then he looked me a question, for all the world like he were askin', "You scared?"

"Suits me," I said, and away we went, leaving the land behind us and soon nothing but sea in all directions.

It put me in mind of when the topsails of last great ship from the City of the Sea went over the horizon leaving us rejects alone, alone, all by ourselves with nothing in sight. Back then, I'd seen the panic rising in their eyes, and I'd told them, "It's easy. Head west into the sunset, and ask where we are when we get there."

I told you that before, didn't I? That's what comes of being old, lad.

Well, getting back to where I was, that were the way I felt when Jim and me headed northeast. It were as if I'd dropped more'n twenty years and was back in me brash-an'-bold youth again, asking for adventure.

Jim and me had a long night, neither of us willing to take a watch below, with the both of us not talking about the unholy great worrisome thought that we was sailing by the luck of the wind. That whole night we didn't say more'n what was needful for watch-keeping, each with one eye on the other by the light of the worthless binnacle. At false dawn the sky lit up enough so's we couldn't see the stars by which we'd been steering, nor nothing else but dark water with the occasional cresting wave. I said not a word but I was gritting me teeth, and over the turned-up collar of his black tarpaulin jacket, Jim was looking ahead like his eyes was gimlets. We sailed on for what seemed like a long time, and then the sun slid up over the horizon ahead of us, pouring golden light right across the still-black sea onto grey, rounded cliffs the like which I hadn't seen since I was aboard *Wetfoot*, looking after a bunch of children, their mums, and half a dozen lubbers all keen to become their lords and masters.

Jim and me looked at each other and grinned. Later, when we was having ourselves a morning mug-up to celebrate our landfall, I found out why he'd been avoiding me probing questions what usually made any new man to the ship start talking about himself, where he came from, where he'd been to, what he'd seen, who was on his last ship — you know, the little drips and drabs that a man puts into words that gives an attentive listener like me a peek into what it is that makes him keep on keeping on.

He waited until the sun was full up and our mugs dead empty. Then he rummaged in his jacket pocket, and pulled out a length of line half as thick as me little finger, looked to make sure I was looking, and with his eyes on mine, took hold of the line like he was going t' haul on it, then brought his hands so's they were facing each other together, finger-and-thumbed with both hands, pulled out two loops with an overhand knot between them. Then, still looking at me, he says:

"You stick his head in the middle, his hands through the loops on either side, pull taught until his wrists are alongside his ears, run the ends down his back, hitch them to his ankles and you've caught yourself a tom-fool."

Which was the very words I'd spoke to a passel of boys and girls aboard *Wetfoot* all them years gone by.

A name came back to me: "James?"

"I answer to Jim," he says.

An' then he starts talking like water pumped out a hose pipe. It were mostly a bit of a jumble, particularly concerning the who and why of it. But by the time we were close enough to make out the shape of the cliffs, I had the beginnings of an understanding of what had happened to Abner's fort after I'd rowed back to *Wetfoot* and the tender mercies of Markab, Enif, and that black-cloaked grand master of the Men of the Sea, Zubin.

Near as I could figure from what came out of Jim's mouth, they hadn't had what you call call an auspicious beginin'. The first winter, they near froze, hungry the whole time. The weakest among them, women and kids of course, never got to see spring. They hadn't harvested much of what little they'd planted when they arrived, and that was on account of they didn't know what they were doin'. Abner thought he did, but what he had them do was mostly wrong, cause he wouldn't listen to nothing that two farmers and three farmers' wives could tell him. Perhaps it was because they all were caught up by believing "in faith, in hope, in loyalty and in peace." Perhaps it were because Abner was too busy using his considerable persuasive charms on an ill-assorted handful of men, a dozen or so recent widows and a bunch of youngsters — all of them seriously messed in the head from what they'd been through. So sure was he of hisself, they did what he told them, the poor fish!

Jim didn't remember much, and what he did was what a boy of eight noticed and took to heart. Like his ma dying. Like being everlastingly hungry. Like being ordered around and occasionally belted upside the head by that square-shaped feller name of Matthew, what I'd met when I cocked a snook under the tarpaulin on the cart-load of guns, and the same feller who'd accused me of dumping the gun wagon. Turned out, Matt was their ace in the hole, 'cause he was a real farmer, and when spring came he left The Fort and got to farming on his own with no advice from Abner to confuse the women and boys he took with him, one of which was Jim. That weren't part of the mighty Abner's plan, but he had to go along with Matt if they was all going to eat reg'lar.

Listening to all of that and a good deal more what I've forgotten took us to where we could see the rocks at the cliff foot, all splashed with spray, and the occasional clump of tough little trees clinging to the top of the headlands. That was when I asked Jim what he had in mind, 'cause after what he'd been saying, it didn't seem such a good idea to sail in all smiles and wish Abner and his happy family a big hello — least not until we had a better idea of which way the wind was blowing ashore.

Jim didn't say nothing, so I sailed the ketch on down the coast until we saw the big bay with Charton at its head. No sooner were we alongside the wharf than Jim says,

"Thank-ee, I'll walk the rest of the way."

"Ho no you don't," I said, and we went to the pub what's right on the wharf. A few mugs of beer and a good meal of land grub later, I got him talking again.

And of course it was all about the girl he'd left behind him.

Eleven

I knew that'd bring you both back for more.

You remember me telling you about the two girls all ripe and ready what Abner dangled in front of me hungry eyes? Well, working it out from what Jim said and didn't say, them girls, and a few others all became "sister wives" for those five fortunate roosters.

Singing Solly had ended up with many wives, but Abner had gone way past unseemly all the way to what old Habakuk would have called immorality, depravity, and a good deal more. Back when I was listening to Al and his favourite sayings, one of them had stuck in me mind: "Woe to him that coveteth an evil covetousness to his house, that he may set his nest on high, that he may be delivered from the power of evil!" Back when Al laid those words on me, I had no idea what Habakuk was going on about, but now I was older and maybe a bit wiser, I thought I did.

According to Jim, all this evil covetousness and unholy carrying on continued for ten - fifteen years, with Abner and Jonas increasing and multiplying what they called The Family. Matthew, he had other ideas, starting with one man, one woman, with no question about which was in charge. Somehow, Jim didn't know how this happened, Abner and Matthew agreed to disagree, and so there was Abner's Fort and Matthew's farm, and neither messed with the other — much.

Time went by, and the boys around Jim's age what I had helped land at The Fort was all growing up. Matthew made most of them into farmers. First of all on his farm, then if they were any good at it, more or less on their own. Sounds fine, don't it? 'Cept that it was Abner what decided who got to start the new farms. An' Abner what said which girls the young men could do their farming with. He hated letting anyone but him decide on a blamed thing.

Abner ruled The Fort, thinking himself the skipper, king, ruler, judge and general all-in-all mucky-muck. But it was Matthew who told the young couples where, what, and how they could do their farming. Jim didn't like that. He'd missed the cut for farms and girls both, and what stung him was he'd figgered he was the first one Matt had chosen, he should have had the first farm, and also be first in line to take over everything when Matthew's farming days were over and it were time for him to get planted.

Well, the years went by, during which Matthew and his wife had no children, which were sad for Matt and supremely tantalizing for Jim, who was sweet on a girl, one of them what *Wetfoot* had landed. According to him, they each was waiting for the other. But that weren't according to how Matt ran his farm or how Abner organized lives. Where Abner was into increasing and multiplyin', square old Matthew was all about one man one wife with no messing about before or after the marriage vows, not in his house, anyway. So Jim and his girl didn't get beyond meanin'ful looks and heavy sighs when he came in from working farmland that still weren't his.

All this and more came at me during supper, and after. When we got back to the ketch, Jim was still banging on about a bunch of people who were only names what I promptly forgot.

I can tell you it all made me proper curious, but I didn't ask about what happened to the skinny girl and her fat little sister, 'cause that was an itch I decided I had to scratch for myself by going t' find out.

So next day I got talking to the publican, and he passed me on to a fisherman, and he talked to the local boatbuilder, and I made a deal on a couple jobs on the ketch what I didn't relish doing meself, starting with the full haul-out, scrape, caulk and a fresh coat of pitch below the water-line, all of which I'd been planning. An' then after I'd taken me savings out from never you mind where, filled a little poke for me belt, put a half-payment in the shipbuilder's hand, and hidden the rest ashore, me and Jim set out to walk to Abner's fort along the cliff-top trail.

It were a footpath just back of the edge, most of the time behind a tangle of shoulder-high bushes — trees, really, what were kept shorter than they wanted to be by the everlasting wind off the sea. It was good walking at first. I could smell the branches that I pushed aside: flat-fronded cedar smelling of an old lady's linen press, prickly spruce like new-sawn lumber, balsam what you can use for a springy scented bed or maybe a pillow if you can find tight-woven cloth, and the occasional pine what had been wind-stunted and twisted out of being a straight and true log what might be made use of for planking a pine-on-oak schooner.

Sometimes the path hooked down into the forest in the lee of the cliffs, sometimes it wandered along the rocky edge where the waves smushed into the rocks a long, long way down, only a false step away. I peered over and down, thinking that I was a whole lot higher than the tallest mast on one of the great ships. I didn't enjoy that part, nor much of the rest of the trip, neither.

You probably heard that sailors don't take much to walkin'. I was fit and strong and all kinds of good looking, but that don't help much when yer feet begin to hurt. Fortunate-like, Jim had the same troubles as me, so what he'd said would be a day's walk, easy, turned into the best part of two days, with an uncomfortable night being chewed by mosquitos in a low-slung, miserable bothy in a clearing where that tangly, wind-stunted forest pulled back from the cliff-top into a grassy clearing. When I first seen the shack, I thought it were just a few logs on top of a pile of stones, but in its lee were a doorway no higher than me shoulder with a door coopered together from salvaged driftwood. Inside, when I laid me down on one of the two slab-wood beds what were only boards set on rocks on the earth floor, I could see stars through holes in the roof, not one of them large enough to do a decent job of letting out the smoke from our miserable excuse for a fire that stung me eyes and made me nose water. Jim said the hut was there fer folk walking the trail in the winter. An' that made a lot of sense, 'cause anyone could see that being caught on that cliff-top path in a snowstorm would be a certain way of never making it to either end. Trouble was that those same benighted travellers had scoured up all the balsam nearby, and then after they'd slept on it, burned it to heat their morning tea, like as not. It weren't winter when we were there, and we both wore our sea-going jackets, but even so, the hut were proper cold and draughty in the early-early hours, when our fire burned down to nothing but the smell of ashes.

Well, next morning, the path took us out of the clearing and inland around a couple little lakes, ponds really, and through a marshy, boggy bit what was home to most of the mosquitos in creation, all of them hungry for our hides, and with no onshore wind to keep them away. Put a foot wrong, and you went down past your ankle into wet, black, forever rotting goop what smelled something between a pile of dead fish and an overflowing privy. Wet to the knees and some miserable, we come out of the bush onto a cart track worn into two brown ruts with a green strip down the middle punched and pocked by the biggest horse-shoe marks I ever seen. Jim said we was near halfway between Abner's fort and Matthew's farm.

"Where you want to go?" I asked him, and he turned to starboard, heading for the farm.

I don't know much about farming, but from all I could see Matthew sure did. We walked a fair piece between cedar-fenced fields growing what back in them days I didn't know the name of, then we came round a bend with cows gawping at us over another fence, and there was a good-looking grey two-storey farmhouse with a big red barn, three or four sheds, a stable with a half door, open for a horse's big head to look out of, and a woodpile long and high enough to keep Matt an' his farmin' crew warm through anything that winter might throw at them. Fer sure, Matthew knew what he was doin', and what's more he must have had all the help he needed for the impressive list of jobs, tasks and chores needful to keep the whole outfit running smooth.

I was heading towards the front door down a neat pathway a'tween beds of herbs and vegables, thinking to ask if we was welcome, when Jim pulled me sleeve, and led me towards the back like anyone but a sailor would know was the place to interrupt what was making a soft rattle and chinking sound I knew as I smelled it was a lot of people eating a meal. Before we got to the door, it opened, and out came a woman carrying two buckets of peelings and scraps what she pitched onto the midden alongside the barn.

"Sal?" said Jim.

"Jimmie?" she said, and drops the buckets. They both stood looking at each other like they'd been carved out of wood and stuck into the ground as posts. That gave me a chance to take a longer look than what's polite when you first meet a woman.

She was tall — taller than me — and she stood to her full height, no slouching or bending her neck so's to look shorter. Healthy and good looking but not showy or flaunting it like some of the women I'd seen in me ports of call. It were her eyes what made me stare: grey-blue above cheeks what were strong and full because of good bones under them — no fat at all. Them eyes plucked at some memory in the back of me head like an itch that's out of reach. She was wearing something in blue, or maybe it were grey, what covered everything except her head, hands and feet. I don't remember 'cause it was what I got used to all the women wearing back then, so's after a while I didn't notice. What got stuck in me mind was how she moved: deliberate, smooth, and light on her feet, like she was almost ready to be dancin'. O' course, when I was staring at her that day, it weren't me she was looking at. She was standing like she'd never move again. Until she did, and at exactly the same moment, Jim did as well. Then he took a step towards her, and she took one back, and then they both froze.

"Maggie's dead," she said, and Jim took a half-step, like he'd been hauled towards her. "I'm next."

"Fer sure?" came out of Jim in a whisper, almost like he was prayin'.

"Looks that way. Soon. Day after tomorrow," she said, and the two of them stood staring like there was a four strand hawser connecting their eyes each to each. "You better go, he's..."

Jim froze again. Right then, a big voice came from inside.

"Who is it?"

"A stranger," she calls out in reply, waving her hand at Jim tellin' him to go, and quick.

"A stranger?" The deep voice repeated, and out the door came a big, square man. I recognized Matthew at once, despite the fact that he'd rounded out since he was aboard *Wetfoot* and gone grey above the ears. His salt-and-pepper beard was cut streight across, just past the second button on his bright blue shirt. Prosperous, is what he was. An' puzzled. He knew he knew me, but he couldn't quite figger out where from, or what to make of me being at his farmhouse. But he knew Jim at first glance, and he wasn't happy about it.

"You," he said, looking at Jim like he was something he'd move with a shovel. "Show this man the way to The Fort. Then leave. Don't come back."

It were a threat. No details; just an unspoken promise of lasting grief from a man with size, strength, and from what Jim had told me, a wealth of bullying experience. Jim only hesitated for the time it took to glance at the woman he'd called Sal, and then he was on his way down the road. Matthew nodded, put one arm around the woman's shoulders, pulling her close like he owned her, and looked down at me — a good trick, seeing as how he was shorter than both me and the woman he was holding.

"Stranger, you come at a time mixed of sorrow that is soon to be turned to joy. Had you arrived this morning, you'd have witnessed us saying our last farewell to my first wife, Margaret. Since you're here, you may stay to be part of the ceremony at The Fort in two days, when Sal and I will wed."

"That'll be right nice," said I, all chipper and cheerful, but I could tell there was something going on in his head under his words, like when the wheel on the ketch twitches in water what's roiled by an undercurrent. While he was talking, he'd been slowly figgering out who I might be, but it was too late to take back his invite, or say anything in front of the woman, who was doing her best to stand straight, in spite of him.

"You'll be wanting to meet with Abner," he said slowly, making it clear that it was what he wanted to happen next. "At The Fort. That way."

He pointed, then turned his broad back on me, let go of Sal's shoulders, gave her a pat on the behind like she was a horse, and went back into the house.

Twelve

I started down the road wondering what I'd gotten meself into, and also wishing I was eating some of the food I'd smelled back at the farm. A few minutes of walking, and I saw Jim, waiting for me in front of a real handsome old house ahead of me, quality in its lines, but in sad need of fresh paint.

"That was going to be Christopher's," said Jim as I came up to him. He's long dead. First winter. Nobody there now."

I didn't say nothin', but I'd seen a flicker of someone taking a cautious peek out one of the front windows. That made me curious, but Jim was going down the road, so I followed him, thinking that he wasn't as up to date as he had been letting on. Soon we passed another house what had fallen in on itself — and as you may have guessed, that's where we're sitting right now, all fixed up by me, and a fair bit of effort it took, too.

Well, we walked a piece further and around a bend in the road, where I saw a great ugly box of a building. Half a dozen five- or six-year old boys were out in the front yard arguing about a ball and knocking each other down. They were in the shadow of the building, what was painted in pelican-puke green, and tricked out with bow windows. 'Tween them, there was pillars holding up two stories worth of balconies above half a dozen wide steps what lead up to a double front door with fretwork curlicues and gingerbread, painted up like a tart's eyebrows in dog-sick-yellow that some bollard-head must have thought looked like gold. There were women and children inside. I could hear at least one baby crying, little'uns being yelled at for something they'd done, and behind it all, the sounds of women working at cookin', washin, cleaning and feeding a passel of children,

"Beautiful, ain't it?" said Jim, making it clear he didn't think so. "Jonas, and his people. Come on, you ain't got no reason to mess with him."

We walked on, with me wondering if Jonas remembered how I'd turned his name against him, until around another bend I saw what they called The Fort, and why. I stopped, so I could take in the ring wall, what you call the ramparts, steep, green and slippery with grass surrounding enough land for one great big stone two-storey house, two barns, three or four sheds, and a cottage, the whole lot of them wide spaced out with lots of short grass keeping them apart. In the middle of was the big house, whitewashed walls two stories high, with two tall, wide chimneys, one at each end. The outbuildings and sheds and barns were connected by bare brown earth paths, the whole lot of them standing in a good-sized stretch of goat-cropped lawn surrounded by the earthworks. I figgered that the other side of the ramparts must have been what I'd looked up at when me and Abner rowed a passel of unhappy settlers to their new home, more'n twenty years gone. Beyond, I could see the glint of water in the great sea bay where we'd made such a bollocks of anchorin', with the cartload of guns going over the side. Way in the distance where it were smudged blue with mist, there was the hills and cliffs what protected the bay from the sea.

While I was looking around, Jim stood beside me, muttering to hisself, looking at the ground. Then he straightened up like he'd made up his mind, told me I could cadge summat to eat in the kitchen of the big house, and scarpered back down the way we'd come.

I let him go, harkening to me empty stomach rumbling and figgering whatever he was up to, it was his business. I followed me nose down to the break in the shoreward side of the ramparts. There weren't anyone around the barns and sheds inside the gap in the ramparts, so I guessed they must all be doing something at the big house. Hoping that it would be food, I walked along the path, around to the eastern end and through the door into the kitchen, like I knew where I was going, all the while pretending I hadn't noticed a boy of about seven running ahead of me, no doubt sent to warn of the stranger at their gates. The little fellow held the door open for me, then ran inside ahead of me down three broad steps into the kitchen-come-dining room.

You two know it well, but to me the space looked like a cross between a big, real clean pub and the mess-room in one of the Great Ships. Two rows of long tables with people sitting on benches, women and girls in grey to the left, and boys and young men in brown to the right, with a skipper's chair at one end of each table for the eldest and a wide gangway down the middle to discourage what you call fraternization a'tween the boys and girls. They all took quick peeks up at me, but nobody was saying nothing even though they had all seen me, a stranger. Forks froze between plate and mouth, spoons stopped scraping bowls, and I never seen so many dead quiet people with downcast heads, all of them working at looking like they was into their vittles, while all the while taking glimpses out the corners of their eyes at me. An' I stood looking back, me mouth watering at all those good land-food smells of meat, gravy, and fresh bread.

At the far end of the room from the door I'd just come through were the tables, workbenches and the ovens where the food was being made and served by a handful of women, all dressed in grey from neck to ankles, their fronts covered by white bib-aprons. They looked up at me a bit nervous-like, but right soon after I gave them me best smile, a sweet-faced, plump lady with flour to her dimpled elbows waved me to an empty table that was set special and important by the window, where all the long tables could see it. Down I sat, feeling a few dozen eyes taking quick looks at me in between mouthfuls.

Right quick for a person that broad in the beam she came back to me elbow. I looked up at her, thinking that if I'd been standing, I'd be looking down on the top of her light-brown-turning-grey-at-the-temples head. We swapped names. She blinked when she heard mine, then she said hers was Miriam. She wasn't at all what I'd seen at first glance. This weren't no fat-and-happy head cook and pastry-maker; for all that she'd brought me little buns warm from the oven, with butter and honey, and a big mug of tea to wash them down.

"You have returned like — like a change in the weather," she said.

Each word she spoke was heavier than its ordinary meaning, for all that her voice was light and calm. There was a look in her grey eyes that saw more than most, and she was in the habit of thinking long and steady about it, too.

"I had the wind at me back," I replied, wondering where we was going.

"As it was when your great ship brought us all to this place," she said very quietly, letting me know she heard me word "back," just like I'd heard her say "return".

"This time I chose me own course," I answered. "And though the ship is smaller, she's mine."

She touched me on the shoulder, gently as a moth landing, and light-footed it back to her oven with her feet rippling the hem of her grey dress.

I'd sat there wondering at what was unsaid in that back-and-forth, and also what it meant to the young people who were still listening so quietly that not a spoon scraped on a plate. Not for long: the clatter soon got started again as they all went back to feeding their faces, while the smell of the warm bread put me straight to work spreading melty butter onto a roll and popping it into me mouth right quick before it dripped on me chin. Me mouth was thinking I'd made it into food heaven when the women who'd been baking and cooking and the like all froze into grey statues, and so did all the folk at the tables.

In came Abner. He looked good. Older, of course, and rounder at the middle, but still fit and healthy. He carried a stout stick with a fancy bright brass handle — mostly for show, I thought, cause he put no weight on it. His white hair was combed just so, his even whiter beard was brushed and trimmed shovel-shaped, like Matthew, but on him it was a whole lot more impressive. He came on like a schooner after a full refit and refurbish, hull scrubbed and painted, brass polished, fresh crisp canvass catching a fair wind. I stopped in mid-chew, and half stood up, polite-like.

He rounded up and stood a pace or two away, looking at me looking at him, out of those black eyes of his that were three points away from scary. I remembered how he'd fixed me with that stare over the fire, back when we first met, and just like then, my feeling that he was somehow unnatural turned into curiosity.

"Angel," he said. "The angel who chose a sailor's duty. What brings you here? Have you returned to fulfill your destiny?"

He gave me a half-smile and a look that took me back to when the two of us were making off with the ferry and getting the horses, wagon and all of his motley crew aboard *Wetfoot.* Except that this time, even while I was feeling his power, part of me was watching him wield it, admiring how he took command of the situation, observing how years of practice had turned raw talent into practiced skill.

"Just co-operating with the inevitable," I said, me mouth still full of food.

He laughed. It was a big, round, friendly laugh, but it was an instant late. He blinked, like he was pretending he wasn't remembering how I'd taken charge of him, back in that fire-lit moment in the forest. I swallowed me mouthful of bun and butter and grinned back like I hadn't noticed nothin'.

"Sit! Sit!" he said, which was all show, 'cause I hadn't really stood up.

Without looking around, he lifted a hand, and Miriam brought more buns and more tea in a big, round, brown teapot. He sat himself down, laid his stick on the table so's I could admire its polished brass head, and smiled, showing lots of still good teeth. He leaned back, like we was mates settling in for a good old yarn about the years what had passed since last we met. And that's exactly what we did, but each of us was watching the other, both of us pretending we was as open, trusting and guileless as I surely had been back then when I was young, spry and trustin'. He rambled on, spinning yarns about the peaceful, contented, community what he'd conjured out of the rag-tag collection of settlers he'd brought north aboard *Wetfoot.*

I watched and listened and admired, like I'd admired him years before. What he didn't know was that I wasn't really admiring him, I was admiring his act, and speculating that behind the smooth flow of his words, he was wond'ring what he was going to do with me. I wasn't about to give him no tips nor suggestions. In between telling me about contented cows and bumper harvests and happy little grand-children, he catches me eye and holds it.

"Where you been all this time, Angel, while we've been building the future in hope, in faith, in loyalty, and in peace?"

"Afloat, mostly," I said, recalling how old Matthew had spouted them same pious words at me aboard *Wetfoot*. Same as then, I doubted they was anything more than hankering after a better world that ain't for real now, nowhere, nor never.

I nodded companionably as Abner's continued his bright-polished tale of twice ten years filled with what he called the turning seasons, the full barns and granaries, and the faithful lives of all who lived and worked for the betterment of The Fort. It were a fine recruiting speech: the sort that gets young and foolish men to step up, sign up and thereby set themselves up for a ship load of hard work, pain and abuse. From time to time, he looked at me like he expected me say 'amen' to his near-to-prayer stuff about hope, faith, loyalty and peace.

While his words were washing over me, I was thinking about the years that had passed since when we met, and what we'd both done in them. I certainly didn't have a story to tell about full barns, happy children, or peaceful living. Mine was scraping and scrabbling to get to the next safe spot, where I weren't looking over me shoulder to avoid the next breaking wave or drunk bastard hankering after what might be in me pocket. There weren't no way I could tell him about all that, and I also wasn't going to let nothing fall about me, or Jim, and still less about a skinny girl and her chubby little sister, leastways until I had a better idea where things was headed.

When the teapot was mostly empty, Abner held up one hand and again wi'out looking around, called for more. A girl came quick as she could without actually running. She was shy, blue-eyed, chubby-faced, not much above thirteen. I smiled at her, the way you do, to be pleasant. Abner saw me, and turned his big head around to stare at her. She looked down, almost like he'd swung that stick of his in her direction.

"Ruth, daughter of Miriam, stand up straight so Angel can see you. And smile."

She did as he told her, but it cost her. Her eyes blinked, her shoulders hunched, and her hands trembled even though she was holding them clenched under her breasts.

Abner nodded, like a man does when his dog sits on command.

"Now fetch more tea and rolls. Off you go!"

He watched her hurry away.

"Nice little piece," he approved, and then his voice changed like Al's did when he spoke the words of poetry he'd memorized. "Thy two breasts are like two young roes that are twins which feed among the lilies." And then he looked at me and raised his shaggy eyebrows and looked after her sideways, like a sailor sighing after a barmaid he'd like to know much better.

"Singing Solly," I said, and then corrected myself. "Song of Songs."

"Very good," he said, and meant it, because I'd surprised him with me erudition — how's that for a good word? — what I'd improved from time to time over the years. Not steady reading, you understand. Just checking out what Al had mentioned back when he'd told me I was too young. Him knowing for sure, as I think about it now, that there was no better way of making me look it up for meself.

"And did you see how her bottom swings her skirt back and forth?"

I stared at him, steady, thinking he was too old and she too young for that kind of … um … appreciation, particularly in front of the girl's ma.

"Looking at something like her kind of peels the years off you, doesn't it?"

Abner smiled as he spoke, like if he had been closer, he'd have nudged me in the ribs with his elbow. He reached for his stick, stood up, hardly leaning on the arms of his chair at all, and dangled his hook.

"There's still room here for an intelligent, active man."

I put me head on one side and scratched it. I remembered the two girls Abner had offered me back in the day, but this felt different, and I didn't care for where it was going.

"I been a long time seafaring," I said. "I'm like a shark: I got to keep moving."

"Before you take to your oars again, why don't you look around for a bit?" His voice changed back to what it was when he was still rambling on about full barns. He'd hauled his wind and gone about so sudden, I wondered if the last few moments had happened. I nibbled his bait.

"Still and all, land food like this here tastes of something I been missing."

An' I let him see me eyes wander over to where the women was busy being busy, all the while keeping an eye on the pair of us.

"Then we will put you in the guest house. You've arrived at a good time. We are about to hold a gathering to solemnize the union of chaste new wives. Special food. You'll enjoy it."

With that, he left me to polish off the buns, what I'd been holding back from cramming into me face. The sweet little girl brought more tea, but she wouldn't look at me, and I was ashamed to look at her.

Thirteen

When it were clear to me that there wouldn't be any more food until supper, I stood up, walked over to where the women were working and asked Miriam if she could point me the way to the guest house. The other women all startled. Their quick, wide-eyed glances were enough for me to figure out that I'd stepped over a boundary like the invisible line that separated the tables a'tween the men and women. Right then, I decided to go slow until I'd found out what the rules were before I broke any more of them.

Miriam spoke to one of the young men who had been watching me from his chair at the head of the nearest table, and he summoned a boy of maybe ten, who led me the hundred or so steps it took across goat-nibbled grass to a stone cottage roofed in grey slate that stood close to the grassy ramparts, not far from where stone stairs led up to the crest, four or five times me hight above.

After the boy had run off, leaving me at the door, I took off me boots, what were still damp from all the walking and wading, left them outside with me socks draped over them to dry, and went in. Nice little cottage it is, too, as you well know. One main room, fireplace, timbered roof arched above, one big window facing away from The Fort, couple of big chairs with arms facing each other across a table, sideboard against the wall with plates, cups and bottles on shelves. I hung me jacket on the peg beside the front door, padded across the floor, leaving damp footmarks in me wake, took a peek through the door at the back into the sleeping room, and fell into the biggest chair in the main room, thinking to sit for a while to make up for that savage pile of rock and boards I'd lain on the night before.

At first, I kept wondering why I'd let Jim's dare take me back to where me life had so nearly changed course, and asking meself what I was doing, messing about with people out of a past I'd long left behind. And as me mind wandered, half-asleep, from time to time I puzzled on how it was that even before Abner came into the room, the women in grey and the men in brown could stay so unnatural silent. And where Jim had got to. And why Miriam and her daughter had been wound up so tight. An' like an itch I couldn't reach I kept getting the creeps from the way Abner quoted old Singing Solly and then fondled that thirteen-year-old child with his eyes. Old Habakuk would have called that a "woe unto you" moment.

Another part of me wished I could get back the feeling Abner put into me when we'd worked together, and after, when he'd offered me those ripe girls, because that were a moment what had come back to me often over the years right about while I was falling asleep, which is what I did next.

Much too soon, there was a knocking at the door. Up I got, gummy eyed from sleeping in the daytime, and there, with an armload of clothes held in front of her, was Miriam. Still half-asleep, I stood aside to let her come in.

"I shouldn't," she said, but in she came anyway, plopped the clothes on the table, and stood looking at me.

"You all of a piece?" I asked.

"I shouldn't," she said, again. Then all of sudden, like she couldn't hold the words back, she started to talk, quietly-quietly, almost to herself, but she wasn't talking like she didn't want to be overheard, the way it was when we talked in the kitchen.

"Matthew's dead."

I must have blinked, 'cause she nodded, her eyes wide.

"He was alive when I saw him earlier today, before I came to your kitchen and you fed me them tasty little rolls."

"After you left, a Watchman fetched me to the Farm. It was a heart attack, they said. I know better. Something long, thin and sharp as a knitting needle had gone in above his left collar bone, straight down into his heart, and back out so slick there was only a little squirt of blood on his shirt."

Her soft little underlip quivered, and she blinked quickly. I got a chair behind her, and she sat, her hands shaking in her lap.

"How do you know?

"I'm the midwife and thanatologist," she said.

"Midwife, I know. But what's a thana-tolo-whatever?"

"The person who makes dead people presentable. I wash bodies, after birth and death. Beginnings and endings. Someone has to."

She didn't say anything for a piece, and then she couldn't stop herself talkin'. When I first met her, she had been rare careful with her words; all thought, no emotion, leastways none on the surface. Now it were the other way around. Once she'd told me that this weren't no ordinary death, she couldn't stop herself from telling me everything she'd heard. It came spilling out that Matthew left the table when there was knocking at the front door. He was only gone for a short time, but when he came back, he staggered into his chair, and fell face down, dead in his dinner. The women called for the Watch, who picked him up, put him in the front room, and sent for Miriam. Heart attack, the watchman told her.

I wanted to know more about who or what the Watch was, but she had the wind in her sails, so I let her go on.

When she arrived at the farm she heard people whispering about poison. As she was getting Matthew ready for viewin' and buryin', she found the hole in him, and in that moment she knew right clear she shouldn't say nothin'. So she fixed old Matt up, and walked back to The Fort to do what Abner had told her to do, which was to bring me some good clothes to wear.

I asked who did it, and why, but she shook her head, her eyes wide with the knowing that she'd probably said too much. When I asked her who else knew, again, her eyes told me how scared she was that she'd told me as much as she had.

"Nobody knows except me and you," she said, "And whoever did it. If you say anything, then they'll know I know, and I'll be next."

I took a breath to argue that she'd be safer if more people knew how it had been done, and then I let it all out. She was right. She had to keep the killer's secret. And so I had to, as well.

"They must be wondering why he'd be healthy one moment and dead the next."

"They think it's Sal who did it because she took one look at him lying face down and ran off. Then one of the Watchmen denounced her as a poisoner."

"Misleading, but right convincing to folk prepared to accept any explanation."

I were trying for wise, but she wasn't attending to me.

"Except that she didn't kill him. The truth doesn't matter to them. They probably think she murdered poor Margaret as well."

I wanted to know more, but all of a sudden, she was up and on her way, desperate to get back to a normal that weren't never going to return. I stood in the doorway, watching her head back to The Fort, her grey skirts rippling as they were kicked up by her heels. Her last words stayed with me.

"You won't say anything."

Fourteen

I sat back down and took stock. I'd been convinced by everything Miriam said, but when she'd gone I found myself asking if she'd been making it all up. When I met her in the kitchen, she'd remembered I'd helped bring them all to The Fort. Then when Matthew was dead and she had reason to think it was murder, she'd told me. Maybe that was because she had to talk to somebody, maybe because she wanted me to do something. But when she left, she'd told me to keep me mouth shut.

I looked down at me bog-stained breeks and wiggled me bare toes, trying to make sense of it all when there was so many gaps in what I'd found out so far.

When we'd first met, Matthew told me that everyone was busy mourning his first wife and getting ready to celebrate when he married his second. So who killed Matt? And why? Now he was dead, that had to mess up the chain of command that kept the farm, The Fort, the family, in fact the whole enterprise on an even keel. Jim had told me Matt was necessary to Abner's Fort, so back then when the farm got started, they must have worked out some kind of an agreement between the two of them, and Jonas as well, which should have guaranteed that none of them would want to do the others any harm.

So why had Abner been fishing fer me to stick around? When he was talking and I was scoffing little new buns, neither of us knew Matthew was dead. It didn't make sense for Abner to want me aboard 'cause they all had good reasons to keep things pretty much as they were. An extra man would disturb the family, upset the balance. Unless that was what he wanted. Maybe Matthew or Jonas was getting uppity. Or Abner thought they were plotting against him. He was surrounded by women all doing his bidding; he seemed confident as a man could be, but what did I know of how he kept his command. I remembered him from back when I'd got them all aboard *Wetfoot* as a man who was absolutely in charge, but enough time had gone by for Matthew and Jonas to become a lot more than leading hands to be ordered around.

I wanted to run after Miriam to ask her when and how and why Abner had told her to take me the clothes that were sitting on the table in front of me, because that had to have been after he knew Matthew was dead.

I picked up the shirt. It was fine white linen, the same quality as Abner wore; and the breeks were soft and supple, not the working clothes worn by the men and boys. If I wore them, I was going to look me best for … what? Abner had said there was a ceremony was planned for the next day, but that was to have been Matthew's wedding, which definitely weren't happening.

Was Abner planning on giving me Matthew's job now that he was dead? I didn't know nothing about farming, but the people doing the work sure did, so a bright feller like me who's used to organizing people could probably fake it until he knew what he was doing.

Or was I being set up to be fingered as the murdering outsider? I'd made the trek along the cliffs 'cause I wanted to know what had happened to Abner and his followers, and more particularly the skinny girl and her little sister, but before I could satisfy me curiosity, I'd heard of a murder and been told a secret that could get deadly for Miriam, and at least right uncomfortable for me. I considered pulling on me boots and heading for the cliff path, except that would make me as much a suspect as the woman what had run off — and besides, I'd never know what happened to the skinny girl.

I was turning all this over in me mind when there was a knock at the door. This time I answered with me bare foot braced to hold it from being shoved open, and me shoulder, arm and left fist full of me knife behind the door.

It were Jonas. He'd filled out around the middle, lost hair on top, added a soft wobbly under-chin, and he'd grown a fat black moustache that hung over his thin-lipped mouth, but he still had the same beaky nose. I stood me ground, wondering if he had it in mind to throw the punches he'd so dearly wanted to let loose back aboard *Wetfoot*.

"Jonas," I said, andj ust to be confusin', put a pleasant smile on me handsome face as I swung the door open.

"Angel," he said, and stuck his hand out. "No hard feelings."

"Water in me wake," I said, matching his tone, but leaving him with his hand in the air.

"Drink with me, Angel," he said, showing me the little stone bottle in his left hand.

"Why not," I said, I took his right hand in mine while folding up me clasp knife in me left and slipping it into me pocket. I let him in, and waved him to the table. We sat down opposite each other, like we were going to play cards, or maybe arm-wrestle. I guessed that me smile was as false as the one that tugged up the corners of his mouth, going nowhere close to his eyes.

He put his flask on the table, I found a couple of mugs, and moved the clothes Marion had brought to a spare chair. He poured, and we both knocked back a couple fingers worth. It did the job, even though it could'a done with a few more years mellowing in the cask.

"What brings you here, Angel?" he asks.

Fair question, so I answered mostly true.

"I was curious about how you folks had done after we left you. An' 'cause I was in the neighbourhood, I decided to drop in."

"I've often thought about you," he began.

Now if he'd taken a run at me, soon as I opened the door, I'd a' believed him, but he hadn't, so I didn't.

Abner sent you?" I asked, reminding him I knew who was master here.

"I make my own decisions, and I've decided you're a man who can be trusted."

I wondered just how he could have come to that conclusion, and tried not to let me eyebrows express me doubts.

"I have information and a proposition," he says, talking like we was two businessmen making a deal.

"I'm listenin'," I said,.

"Matthew's dead."

"In'erestin'," I said, behind me mug. "He was live enough to talk to me only three-four hours ago."

"Face down in his mashed potatoes," said Jonas with a touch more satisfaction than I'd have expected.

"Too much high living?"

He swigged, ignoring me question.

"Looks like Sal poisoned him. She ran off."

"Ain't she the one he was s'posed to wed?"

"She was. More important, we're a man short."

He pushed his flask across the table, but I didn't touch it.

"Surely there's some smart young farmer who can … um … take the reins?"

"Three who'd like to, but none of them as able as Matthew." He paused and repeated himself. "Able. Your name, isn't it? And didn't you say … take the reins? Like when you got the horses onto the boat…"

"I worked with Abner. I'm a sailor, not a farmer. What I know about horses is that you get aboard from the port side, facing aft."

He didn't get it, but that didn't stop him grinning as if he did, before going on making his pitch.

"So… not a farmer, then. Pity. Abner thought you could help us all again. And yourself."

I took another sip, just enough to tingle me tongue. So, I thought. Abner sent you? Or you want me to think Abner sent you?

"Jonas, what do you do exactly?" I asked.

"Facilitate. Expedite. Negotiate."

Abner sent you, I decided. You're Abner's dogsbody. The tail what thinks it wags the dog. I looked at him real steady and stayed quiet. A part of me was still kinda hankered after the feeling Abner put into me when we'd worked together, so I must have looked like I was thinking it over. But instead of pressing his advantage, he squirmed in his chair, leaned forward, lowered his voice and took another tack at softening me up.

"Just between us, should you decide not to join us, I have a feeling you're a man who might be interested in a profitable arrangement."

Silence seemed to be working well for me, so I let him go on.

"You got here in your own boat."

"Nope. I walked in."

"But you got a boat in Charton."

He was working that hard I had to give him a nod.

"Listen," he said. "You, me and your boat, we could get into trade."

He poured another two fingers for the both of us, and words bubbled out of him with all the forthright, honest, truthfulness of a man selling old rope. He glowed enthusiasm like sunshine came out of his eyes. He was a man with an extra-special never-been-thought-of-before idea. Except I was listening to a feller who had spent the past twenty years cooped up in a weird little settlement on the ragged edge of nowhere, who was telling me that there was money in trade. He talked to me about the excellence of The Fort's fish, honey, preserves, weaving, baskets, carving, pottery, candles, needlework, cider, whisky, and a bunch of other stuff, all of which was made in every town, port or village I've ever been into. I don't think me face changed, although inside I was shaking me head in wonderment that a man could be that simple.

When I didn't clap me hands together in glee, eventually he ran down like a clock that's due for a winding. I held me face blank, but after a while I couldn't stand it a moment longer.

"What are you looking to get that you ain't got now?"

"Steel, tools, cotton, clocks, seed, glass, …"

"An' yer planning to pay for stuff like that with fish, weaving, pottery, carving, baskets, and whisky? Which is what everyone already has — and thinks they can do better than anywhere else?"

He sat there blinking at me, like me words had slapped him in the face with a fish. So I hit him again.

"And just what do I get out of the deal?"

"You'd get … you'd get a piece of … you'd profit by…"

"Jonas, I'll go on trading the way I been trading for the past near-on twenty years. I'll sell you what I got that you want, I'll buy what of yours I think I can sell. I deal at the dock."

"Well then, perhaps we could come to a mutually satisfactory arrangement…" he said hopefully.

"Is that we meaning you, or we meaning you'n Abner and all his faithful flock?"

"Ah … they would all profit from your active participation in the conduct of The Fort's life and livelihood, but as for the trading, well, that would be just you 'n me."

I nodded. I understood. He was in it for himself.

"Then everything that goes into or out of me ship has to be backpacked along that miserable path along the cliffs to Charton, 'cause I'm guessing you don't want me sailing into the bay here to load up in front of Abner and all them womenfolk."

"Ah, yes … for now."

Interestin', I thought to meself. All them hints about needing someone to be taking over from Matthew was likely Abner's idea, but Jonas is figgering some way of going behind Abner's back, scuppering his deal and making his own. It's funny. I'd missed the mutiny aboard me own ship, but I sure was sniffing it out real easy ashore, and that made me feel right smart — smarter than I really was.

"If you go back and tell him that I'm open to his offer — o'course without mentioning your grand idea, what's in it for you? "

He stood, headed for the door, then turned around and pointed that great nose directly at me.

"Do it my way, you still get to visit, and maybe meet up with some of the women who … lack regular company. You do it Abner's way, all you'd get would bc Sal. Mark you, she knows more about the when, where, and how of farming than Matthew did, so you'd have no problem heading up the farms. Nice body, too. Word is, you'll be the first. Treat her right, and maybe she could run things while you are away, doing our business, on your boat."

"Well then," said I, and plays for time. "Maybe I shouldn't be hasty."

"Think it over. Either way, you win. Keep the whisky."

He got up and headed for the door.

So I slid Jonas out the door on a few more soft and soapy words that didn't let on that I'd sussed out his plans, and seen there was no way any of them would work. I watched his back going away down the path to the big buildin', and I grinned to meself, thinking how much smarter than him I was.

Like old Al said, "Pride goeth before a fall."

Fifteen

So now you're probably wondering if I was thinking to rat Jonas out to Abner, aren't you? Well, you'll have to wait, 'cause I have a couple more upwind tacks afore we get to the downwind run to the end of me story.

I shifted into the new pair of blue breeks from Abner, lit the candle on the table and was contemplating another swallow of Jonas' whisky, when there was a tap, tap, tap at the door again.

"Wait a bit," I sung out, and tippie-toed me way to the door, mouse-quiet in me bare feet, threw open the door so that the light was in whoever's eyes, seized a handful of shirt-front and pulled. I had me other fist back and ready when I saw what I'd grabbed. An' then I let go and started blathering apologies, 'cause me hand was in the chest of a tall, bright-eyed woman. The day was sloping down towards evening, and we was in the shadow of the ramparts, but there was still light enough for me to see her face, even if it were a bit late.

I was looking at the stubborn, skinny girl all grown up. I stood there in the door like I'd been hit up the back of the neck by the main boom jibing. There was streaks of grey in her copper-coloured hair, but her eyes were what I saw, and they were still blue-green like the open sea.

"I'm Michael," she said, and all I could do was nod. "You're Angel from *Tidewalker*. I'm looking for my sister, Sarah."

And with that, I finally glommed onto the bleeding obvious that the Sarah who was also Sal and Sally, once was the little one with her thumb in her mouth.

"Not anymore. I'm on me own. No Sarah here."

"I know that. Are you going to let me in? Because if I stand here much longer, someone's going to see, and that won't be good."

In she came, me with me mouth still hanging open.

Michael looked at me steady.

"Angel, will you help us, again?"

I looked back at her like I'd never look away, and nodded. She shied back, like a horse does when you come at him with a halter.

"Just like that? Are you foolish? Without knowing anything about what you're getting into?"

Her eyes narrowed and the lashes flickered like spindrift flying off breaking waves. She was fierce, like she had been when she was a skinny girl looking after her little sister.

"Tell me," I said.

We stood near the window, me facing the shadow of the rampart, her with the candle lighting one side of her face. I found meself taking a half step to see her better. This time, she didn't flinch.

"Matthew is dead. Everyone thinks Sarah did it. But it wasn't her, it was Jim, and now he's run off with her."

From bride to be to murderer to woman on the run in less than five hours, I thought, and me face must have shown it.

"He couldn't have done it, he was with me," I said.

It took me a moment, but once I'd heard what I'd said, I knew I was wrong. Jim left me on me way to The Fort. He had time to double back. I didn't say anything, but me face must have shown that I was having second thoughts, even as she was setting me right.

"I was there and saw it happen. I heard most of what was said out the back door, too. After Matthew sent Jim and you on your way to see Abner, he went back to the table to finish his meal. Then there was a knock at the front door, and because Abner's the only person who comes in that way, Matthew got up from the table and went to meet him. He was only gone for a moment, when he came back alone, staggered into his chair, and fell face down into his plate. I was serving the person next to him. I bent over and saw his eyes, and I knew he was dead. When I opened my mouth, Watcher Ned stood up, pointed at Sarah and yelled, "Murderer! Murderer! I denounce thee!" She ran."

The shadows on Michael's face shifted, and I saw her frown with the effort of keeping control. I was impressed. First with what she said, and just as much that she'd been able to say it so matter-of-factly. So I didn't say the first thing in me head, which was that running was the stupidest thing Sarah could have done, and instead asked what could possibly make the Watcher think that she'd done the deed. Michael stayed all cool and calm, but I could see it was costing her.

"Ned must have heard Jim talking to Sarah and Matthew. Now the rest of the Watchers are spreading the rumour that she killed Matthew so that Jim would marry her and take over Matthew's farm."

I nodded. Her head tipped to the right, the shadows shifting, the light catching one eye.

"You don't seem surprised," she said.

"I guessed there had to some way Abner gets to know who's talking to whom about what. You just told me that there's spies, rumour-mongers and enforcers what you call Watchers. And there's runners — boys to carry messages."

"When did you come to know that?"

"There was a boy what ran ahead of me when I was walking to The Fort. Nobody blinked an eye when I arrived. They were curious, that's for certain sure, but nobody was surprised that a perfect stranger had blown into the kitchen."

She nodded, and again the shadows flowed across her face.

"By now everyone has heard that Sarah's a murderer. All Abner has to do is pass judgement at the Gathering."

That took me aback. "Abner's decided? Just like that? Don't there have to be a finding out of what happened ... a hearing ... a trial?"

"There weren't any men there," said Sarah.

"There was at least one," I said. "You just told me his name ... Watcher Ned."

"Watchers don't speak at Gatherings," said Sarah. "They tell Abner in secret, he decides, and what he says, goes."

"None of the women gets to say anything?"

She shook her head.

"Yer jokin'," I said, but I could see from her face that she wasn't.

"Abner's is … persuasive."

"I remember. He made me feel part of something important."

"He dangled two ripe young women in front of your drooling mouth."

"I didn't drool."

"You ogled. Then you left."

"I came back," I said.

"A bit late."

"I was curious …"

We both looked at each other, like we'd come out of the back-and-forth pretty much even. I even saw the flicker of a smile lift one corner of her mouth, but it could have been the candle-light.

"Is Abner the same as you remember?" Michael asked, her voice calm, her head level, her eyes glinting in the shadow of her brows.

"He's older," I said.

She raised an eyebrow, and I saw one sea-green eye looking right into me.

"So?" she asked.

So I went on, taking time to think, feeling me way as I went.

"When I first met him, he was in command, but he was making it up as he went along. I saw that he was all fired up 'cause he'd discovered the power to get people to do what he told them. Now, he's set in his ways. He's maintaining authority. He's practicing the fine art of keeping everyone in the habit of obeyin'."

That sea-green eye softened, somehow.

"Will you go on obeying him?"

"I never started. We began with me telling him what had to be done, and he did it. It felt like we were partners."

Michael took me point, but didn't let me get away with it.

"That's how he's been controlling Matthew, Jonas and the Watchers. He makes them think they're cooperating with him, that the Watchers are also theirs. They're not. They're Abner's. Matthew and Jonas are puppets. Abner keeps them under his thumb, because he decides where the women go."

"Like Sarah?"

"All part of the plan, Abner's plan. Everyone knew Matthew's wife would die soon. She'd had six miscarriages that we knew about. Sarah had been keeping the farming records for more than ten years. Abner might as well have announced that Sarah was the next wife. She couldn't see a way out."

"Hold on now," I said. "Jim told me that Matthew walked out of The Fort with his one and only wife after the first winter to take charge of farming. He's not beholden to Abner, he's…"

"He's dead," said Michael, "And that gives Abner total control, In hope, in faith, in loyalty, and in peace. She spoke through clenched teeth.

"Words to live by," I said.

"It's not words," said Michael. "It's a spell."

"I got all night," I said. "Eddicate me."

So with me nodding like a baby's toy, even when I wasn't taking in all the details, Michael up-ended, pitch-poled and capsized what was left of how I'd felt when Abner 'n me was working together back when I'd taken that sad little rag-tag procession of women and children through the night all those years before.

According to Michael, in the first winter when they was all huddled up in The Fort trying to keep warm, they'd all been nicely paired off by Abner, who split the mothers with children among five men. The women accepted the partners that they'd been dealt, because what else could they do? But there were spare women, and that led to some swapping and changing going on during those long, cold, hungry winter nights.

All of it, in hope, in faith, in loyalty, and in peace.

One of the men, Christopher, who I didn't even notice aboard *Tidewalker*, turned out to be even more of a blue-sky, rainbow-chasing re-make-the-world-only-better dreamer than Abner. Turned out later, it was him what loosed the holding down ropes on the cartload of guns because he didn't want nobody to have them. Didn't matter to him that they were payment for passage what had to be paid again out of Abner's pocket. That Christopher feller had the hope and faith part, he overdid it on peace, but where he was most lacking was in the loyalty department, and that was what Abner craved most.

Well, one dark night that first winter, little Chris bragged about what he'd done into his pillow, and the woman what was sharing the pillow told all on Abner's pillow a couple nights later. When Abner heard, he jumped out of bed, picked up his stick and waxed great wrath in a creditable imitation of old Holy. He dragged Christopher out of his bed, and the smiting what Abner did to him was noisy, bloody and final. Then the only men in The Fort were Abner, Matthew, Jonas, and a feller name of John who everyone but his widow forgot after he didn't make it through the winter.

And so, in hope, in faith, in loyalty to Abner's will and whim, and in his righteously enforced peace they struggled through to spring, which was when Matt moved into an old farmhouse just out of sight of The Fort with the woman he'd picked and then stuck to, 'cause, like I told you before, he was of the one-man-one-woman-and-no-messing-about school of thought. He also took with him some of the older boys, including Jim. So as they began their second year, there was Abner who was like the boss whale, and Jonas who was not exactly inside the whale, but hanging around real close to pick up whatever the whale might let fall, which practically speaking were the women Abner didn't care for, didn't want, had gotten pregnant and he had grown tired of. This were an arrangement about which old

Habakkuk, or Micah, or Jeremiah might have said," Woe unto him that mucketh about, for it never worketh out the way he expected."

Anyway, Abner and Jonas found that they still hadn't got it quite right, and so because there were more women than men, they shuffled the deck and tried again until they'd each got a main wife who was more or less permanent, and two or three what they called "sister wives," whose position was a good deal more fluid.

And to ensure that hope, faith, loyalty, and peace got observed to his liking, Abner made the older boys that were, and in time the boys who followed, into either farmers or watchers, each with a girl to keep him company. And that solved the problem of boys who'd arrived on *Wetfoot*, as well as girls like Sophie and Imogene, me little temptresses. However, it completely left young Jim out of the whole arrangement, what must have made him more'n a little bit tetchy, an' led to a ruckus at the end of which Matthew showed him the door, and Abner had him marched off the premises.

I asked Michael why the women stayed. Silly question, really. It was fear. Fear had made them join Abner's caravan, and fear of whatever might be over the hill kept them in The Fort. It was fear for themselves, for their children, and pretty soon, fear for the babies that Abner and Jonas so generously gave them. Abner held them all together, convinced them they was family by his look, his presence, his voice of command, his unshakable belief in his own rightness, not to mention the memory of that skull-busting moment when Christopher didn't survive the smiting. And when memories of the Wrath of Abner faded, there was the Watchers to enforce Abner's will, which was a nice way of saying that they bullied children and raped uncooperative women and girls.

I wasn't following everything Michael said, but what I lacked in understanding, I made up in conviction that what had happened to the women shouldn't have happened to nobody. This was deep depravity, and just damn bad sense, as well. Me Da weren't no saint, but he wasn't hankering to make his will law over a growing little village mostly composed of his wives and children, still less to maintain a squad of bully-boys to control every last person there.

I had a bunch of questions I wanted to ask, starting with the delicate matter of if Michael and Sarah had become wives or sister-wives, and if not, how they'd managed it, but off in The Fort a bell started ringing.

"Evening curfew?" I asked

The bell went on ringing.

"That's not curfew. They're raising a search for Sarah and Jim," said Michael. "I have to go."

"I think know where they're going," I said.

"Tell me," she said.

"If I was them, I'd head for me boat," I said. "But they ain't had enough time to make it all the way. Right now, it's a fair bet they're spending the night in the bothy."

"Then I'll be back very soon," she says, and off she goes into the early evenin'.

An' that's where I'm going to leave you, till tomorrow.

Sixteen

Michael hadn't been gone longer than it takes me to tell you when I heard bang, bang, bang on the door, and then a sort of a mumble, like when some two are deciding on what to do next. The mumble was too low to be a woman's voice, so I opened the latch cautious-like, and a good thing I had one foot against the door, 'cause there were two of the Watch. They were good-sized young men wearing matching brown breeks, shirts, and jerkins, hair to their collars, silly moustaches, and stupid expressions on their faces. I knew what to expect even before I clocked the short and nasty club one of them was playing with — you know, that tap, tap, tap against the side of his leg, just like every last Watchman everywhere. They all go to the same bullying school, y'know.

Well, when I'd dealt with them …

What's that? You want to know how? You too, lass?

All right then, here's the long of it.

First off, I gave them me warmest smile, and greeted them with a "Good evening gentlemen, is there something I can do for you?"

Watchman Number One, the blonde one with the club, thought that was real funny. He grinned back at me, took a breath to say something, couldn't find the words, and so came right on in, but not with the swaggering entrance he'd planned. While his brain was still getting steerage way, I stepped out into his face, grabbed two handfuls of hair and ears on both sides, and yanked him downwards through the doorway.

He arrived in the cabin head first, looking down at where me knee was coming up. Then as I stepped aside, and he went went face-forward onto the deck, I slammed the door closed, nearly hitting the other feller's nose. Then I put me heel into Watcher One's short ribs, flattening him out so's I could tie him up, hands together upside his back, with the length of line I keep in me breeks, along with me clasp knife.

Yer never know when a short length of heavy twine's going to come in handy.

That done, and Watcher One relieved of his club — not wi'out a short tap to the back of his head, right where the skull leaves off and the backbone begins — it were time for Watcher Two, who were all keen to come to the party, but couldn't because his mate's feet were against the bottom of the door, holding it mostly shut. The only part of Watcher Two that appeared where I could see them was his fingers, curled around the door at a most convenient height for me to take a good swing at them with Watcher One's club.

Now up to now, neither of them had said anything much except for grunts, but there were a loud, satisfying yelp as Watcher Two pulled his hand back, followed by some cursing that I won't offend your ears by repeatin', lass. As he was making free with a few short, sharp, heartfelt words, I heard his big boots take two - three steps back, preparing hisself for the damn-foolishest thing he could do.

He intended to charge the door, shoulder down, but he only brushed it with his arm as he went by me, 'cause I'd opened it. He were off balance when he lurched across the doorstep, stumbling as he tried to straighten up, staggering when he turned to come at me, all of which hustle and bustle were asking much more than he had the smarts to organize. He tripped over his mate, making himself obligin'ly ready for me to administer a sturdy swipe to his right ear with the club I'd borrowed. That made him lie down beside — well, mostly on top of — Watcher One, who was making the little groaning and snuffling noises what people do when they've planted their face into the floorboards and can't get up 'cause their hands are tied.

Thinking to meself that from now on I'd carry two lengths of line in me pocket, I pulled the belt out of the breeks Abner had sent, and used it on Watcher Two's wrists. I flipped him over, sat on his chest, and tenderly swept his black hair out of his eyes with that right handy club.

Then Watcher Two and me had a nice little chat, to which Watcher One contributed the occasional grunt, me having stuffed the tail of his shirt into his mouth, where it did double duty of mopping up some of the blood from his nose and stopping him from talkin'.

After Watcher Two had told me more than he planned about how and why Jonas had sent them, I dragged them into the back room, rolled them up into two neat blanket parcels, tied up with ripped-up pieces of sheet, which also came handy to stifle their lamentations and woe.

There. That's how I took them down, but before y' get lost in admiration, let me repeat: pride goeth before a fall, though I wasn't thinking that at the time, being so chuffed at me own prowess, intelligence and general overall handiness.

So there I was, all puffed up with a towering sense of me own achievement, when a light tap, tap, tap at the door told me Michael was back. So off I swaggered to let her in. When I opened the door, her whisper came to me from real close.

"Two of the Watch are missing…"

I couldn't see her at first, 'cause she was standing right next the door in a black or maybe dark blue cloak that went all the way up and over her head in a wide hood, and right the way to the ground at her feet. The hem brushed me bare foot as she stepped past me. When she turned, I saw her face like it was hanging in the air. The hood hid her hair, the cloak falling from her shoulders to the floor.

I barely got the door closed behind her before me pride got the better of me mouth and I started to boast.

"They're here," I said, "Resting comfortably in the back room."

"Both of them?"

I gave her smug grin and a nod. She didn't seem a bit impressed.

"You want to see who Jonas sent me?" I asked, fishing for a compliment.

We were standing close together by the door. She turned back her hood and the candle-light made little gleams in her hair.

"Jonas?" she said scornfully. "The Watch are Abner's."

"Really?" I said. "I figgered it had to be Jonas who sent them when he got to thinking that I could rat him out to Abner as the scheemin', backstabbing bastard that he so surely is."

She put her head a little on one side and looked at me out of those sea-bright eyes.

"So Jonas came here to do a deal on the side."

I nodded.

"He's hankering after the untold riches what he thinks will come to him from trading what The Fort makes for what The Fort wants."

"I doubt we produce much that other communities might be willing to …" she began.

"S' what I told him."

"Then you told him his idea was stupid," she said.

"Pretty much. Yes."

"Then you could be right about the Watch. Jonas could have talked them into chasing you off, perhaps even you having an unfortunate accident.… But now you've spoiled their plan, it doesn't matter, because it won't be long until someone comes looking for them, and then.…"

"So far, so good," I said all cheerful.

"Let me see them."

We went into the back room and she looked me Watcher-parcels over. They were alive and squirming around a bit, but there wasn't a lot t' look at except for staring eyes and tufts of hair. She stood over them in her black cloak like an avenging angel of doom, then hauled back her boot and kicked each of them in the ribs. Hard.

"You cannot believe how long I have wanted to do that," she said. "The one with black hair is Stan, Jonas 'watcher, the other one is Ned from the farm. I've seen too many women they've raped and children they've beaten."

"So there's one more to go," I said, all cheerful.

"You were lucky. These are the stupid ones. Fred, Abner's watcher won't be so easy. He's smart enough to come to the same conclusion you did. We have to find Sarah and James before he kills the pair of them, and we don't have much time."

And so we set off together.

I'll keep the next bit waiting till you come back tomorrow. Bringing some more of that cider with you, if you please, lass.

Seventeen

Thank'ee. That sure is a right tasty batch. Where were we? Right. Heading for Charton.

I put on me boots and me jacket, threaded me old belt into me new breeks, she blew out the candles, and we snuck out the door and took a look around. The sky was still bright overhead, but the shadow of the ramparts was doing a fair imitation of night. Across the lawn, yellow light spilled out the windows at the kitchen end of the big white building, and up top as well where Michael told me the young girls' dormitory was. More importantly, the main gate had lanterns on either side, and as I watched, one of them moved towards the other — sure sign someone was doing sentry-go.

I stood there, getting me bearings, letting me eyes adjust, wondering what's next. I'd known it was going to a neat trick for us to walk out the main gate and wander off down the road past Jonas' place, but now it had gotten much too dark for me to find the turn-off towards Charton, leaving aside how we were going to wade through the bog, get around the ponds, and most of all, avoid taking a header off the cliff-top.

"Umm, Michael," I whispered. "We agreed on where Jim and Sarah are likely headed, but it ain't exactly clear to me how we're going t' follow them in the dark. If I were aboard me boat, and there wasn't a whole lot of trees and stuff in the way, I'd plot a compass course — no, that's wrong. Around here, I couldn't, on account of because…"

Her fingers grabbed me arm, stopping me in mid-ramble. She breathed "Hush," against me ear, and then. "Here, hold this."

As me fingers closed around her cloak, the smell of cedar wafted out of its folds, and mixed in and behind that, the scent of her. It went straight to me brain and shut down all me thoughts at once. Then she moved, and like a baby hanging onto his mother's skirt, I tagged along behind.

We set off around the back of the cottage, so's it was between us and everyone else. After maybe ten or twelve cautious steps in the dark, she stopped and turned towards the ramparts, what were now close enough fer me to smell wet stone and moss. I couldn't see nothing ahead of me.

"Steps," she whispers.

Up we went, her flowing up like it weren't no problem to climb in pitch dark, me with one hand down on the next-but-two steps above me feet, feeling me way. The steps were stone, and wide enough, but they were ground down in the middle from all the feet that had been up and down them over the years, even before I helped land Abner and his gang on the water side of the earthworks I was climbing.

"Keep low."

Her words reached me as the hand I'd been feeling ahead with didn't find nothin', and I pitched forward onto me knees.

"Good."

It was the first time she'd approved anything I'd done, and it had been an accident.

I crawled onto the top, and all at once, I had eyes again. They didn't tell me much except that a powerful long way below me starlight was faintly flickering on the water of the bay. I was looking down at where I'd looked up from, the day I landed Michael and Sarah. I knew that the path zig-zagged, but I couldn't see nothin', even if I used the lookout's trick of swinging me head back and forth so I looked out the side of me eyes.

"Hold it right there," she whispered.

So that's what I did, crouching on me hands and knees. In front and below me something moved, and I figgered it must be her, there being nobody else around. I heard a scratching noise. Then I was blinking at a patch of path two strides away and one down from me. There was just enough light for me to see her boots below a wavering outline of black that had to be her cloak.

"Put a hand on my shoulder."

I slithered over the edge feet first, felt the path under me, stood up, tried not to think of how far I had to fall if I tripped, reached out and down to where I figgered her shoulder must be.

"That's my head."

I wanted t'say I was sorry, ask where we were going, talk about what she had in mind — just talk to hear her say something back, but

I knew the way sound carries in the open, so I kept me trap shut as we zigged and zagged down towards the water. I caught a quick glance at her face when she blew out the light in her lantern. Her eyes were shut so's she wouldn't look into the flame and go night-blind.

"Now you lead," she whispered. "There'll be good footing if we stay between the tideline and the water."

"I don't know where…" I began.

"Just walk. I don't want to use the lantern when we're in plain sight. There'll be people looking for Sarah and James. Easy for anyone to see a lantern along the waterline. When we get to the stream, I'll take over."

"Why don't you …"

"Because you're a man, and can see better in the dark than I do."

I started walking, and she followed. Above, stars prickled in the spaces between clouds, and I figgered we was heading south. A soft breeze blew the scent of growing things out of the black shape of forest to the east.

"Yer fooling me ain'tcha?"

"Fact. Most men see better in low light than women, most women see more colour than men."

"How do you know?"

"Because I read books."

I slowed down to step over a piece of driftwood. So did she, but more cautiously. I was thinking to boast about how I read books too, but I was concentrating on where we was going, so I grunted out one word.

"Why?"

"Because I'm The Fort's healer."

I stumbled, got me feet going again, and cast me mind back to how they'd nearly left her and her sister behind on that other night journey, years ago.

"How'd that happen?"

"The man who was supposed to do the job died."

"Christopher? The feller what Abner whacked?"

"No, John. He'd had some training, and he packed enough medical equipment, supplies and books to get us started. Over that first winter, we found more books at The Fort. When he died, I took over the job."

"Weren't you …um … sort of young?"

"I was thirteen. My mother had been a midwife, and I'd helped her twice, so when Abner panicked and ran off halfway through a delivery, I took over. Mother and daughter both lived, no thanks to his clumsy efforts. A few days later, one of the boys cut his hand and I stitched it up. After that…"

It was her turn to stumble. I hesitated, she recovered, and we went on. I wanted to keep on hearing her voice over me shoulder.

"You were all by yourself?"

"Sarah helped. She started off fetching and carrying for me. When she was five she was gathering herbs, winding bandages, making beds. By the time she was sixteen, we'd both learned a lot, some of it from books, some from making it up as we went along. We were lucky at first, so when there were things I couldn't do, people understood. Those who died were pretty clearly not my fault, and so gradually people trusted me."

I didn't say, "So that's why you and Sarah aren't wives or sister wives," but the thought was so loud in me mind, for a moment I wondered if I'd spoken out loud. We walked on along the beach in the gloom, slowing down for shadows from the occasional tree growing close to the shoreline. For a while there was only the sound of our feet scrunching on small stones and shingle. Then there was a trickling sound, what I heard too late. I stopped right quick, one boot in icy-cold stream water and the other behind me ashore. She ran into me. I stayed standing up as she steadied herself with a hand on me shoulder. I felt her breath on me neck.

"This is where we turn east into the woods. The path is somewhat bumpy as we go up into the woods, I'll light the lantern and go first."

She was right about the bumps. With her lantern ahead of me to see where to put our feet, we climbed up a steep path carved into the forest when the spring run-off turned the summer trickle into a torrent. We could hear the little stream nearby, tinkling and splashing down the hillside, as we picked our way around head-sized rocks, over tree-roots and under hanging boughs. Occasionally, we had to cross from one side of the stream to the other on stepping-stones that wibbled under our feet. Up we went for what seemed like half the night until we came up out of the trees onto the cliff path.

That's when we saw the campfire.

And what happened there, I'll tell you tomorrow.

Eighteen

I knew that would get you. It's a trick old Al used to get me to come back for more.

First thing Michael did was blow out the lantern. So there we were in the dark, listening real hard. Then very softly, hands-and-knees, we crept towards the light, following a path away from the cliff-edge, down into a thicket of wind-stunted pines. Michael didn't have to tell me to keep me mouth shut.

Lying side by each on soft pine needles, we peeked out under the lowest branches. We was looking eastwards into a pool of yellow, flickering light. What we saw was a good sized watch-fire, much more than you'd build to heat a pannikin of water or fry up a couple rashers of bacon, but short of a full-blown bonfire. It lit the clearing, letting us see the low outline of the bothy where I'd spent that seriously uncomfortable night. The trees all around were blacker than the sky above, what was prickly with stars right down to their tops. Downslope from the bothy was the merest suggestion of a gap where the path led towards the boggy bit and the little lakes.

As we watched, what I'd first thought was a rock got up and turned into a man, who threw a log into the fire. The hot red centre crackled, sparks coiled into the sky and the flames flared. Michael rolled close and whispered in me ear.

"It's James. But I can't see Sarah."

"Maybe she's in the bothy," I whispered back. "There ain't nobody else…"

And then there was.

He was big, and he came up out of the darkness moving fast and quiet, heading for Jim, who had sat back down facing his fire. I took a breath to shout a warning, and then left me mouth open, watching the man's arm go up as he ran at Jim's back. For a moment, all I could see was a black shape made of two men's bodies — no telling who was who. A knife blade gleamed, but it was dropping out of the man's upraised hand, flickering as it fell into the fire. Then the shape turned into one man standing alone, with a long knife gleaming in the red light.

It was all over so quick that Michael and me hadn't had time to even think about moving. Jim must have seen his attacker before we did, but he hadn't let on. He'd waited until the man was almost over him, then he half-stood, twisted around and drove a long, narrow blade up under that raised arm, deep in below the ribs.

A long, narrow blade. Same as offed Matthew. The right length to hide in a sleeve, the right weight to make a tarpaulin jacket thump on the deck of me ketch.

An' the skill that comes from experience.

"Jim's a killer," I said out loud.

"Observant."

Michael's whisper was serious sarcastic.

"Why didn't you say …" I began, and then thought back. I'd defended Jim, given him an alibi that held no water, as Michael knew full well at the time.

"Why did Sarah….?" I whispered.

"He kidnapped her, Angel. Try to catch up."

"Why didn't you tell me …?"

I began, and then shut up. Jim was standing up again, rolling the body downhill, out of the firelight.

"Michael, if I go say hello to Jim like I just arrived down the path, he'll be looking at me, and you can sneak in the door of the bothy, like you was planning to do before Jim…"

"No. He'll kill you. And maybe Sarah. He's crazy."

"But Sarah…" I began.

"Sarah's most likely tied up in the bothy. Maybe even asleep after all she's gone through today."

"How can you be sure?" I whispered.

She spoke as we watched Jim rolling the corpse into the bushes.

"James hated Matthew for chasing him off, years ago. He came back to get even, get control of Sarah, and maybe take over the farm as well. He's making it up as he goes along. He's obsessed with Sarah. Always has been. He thinks what he feels is love, so it's unlikely he's harmed her. But if you rush in, who knows what he'll do. Killing Matthew was a huge risk, but one he might get away with. Now he's killed Abner's watcher Fred as well, he'll have to go on killing anyone who gets in his way until ..."

"Til he sails off with her in me boat."

"Exactly."

I sucked me teeth, thinking. I'd swallowed Jim's twisted story hook, line, and sinker. Never occurred to me that Sarah was scared when they'd met in Matthew's farm yard. I'd thought I'd seen the shared yearning of parted lovers, but that was a story I'd made up, and it blinded me to what was really going on. It was fear, not love in Sarah's eyes as she chose words to calm both Jim and Matthew from the deadly fight that they was on the edge of starting in front of me.

I'd seen it all, but misunderstood completely. Believing it were romance for two, I didn't see it were one man's obsession. Nothin', not even the years gone by, could shake Jim's conviction that Sarah was his. He had doubled back, gone in through the front door like Abner always did, surprised Matthew, stabbed him, shoved him back into the kitchen, where farmer Matt had staggered into his chair and died in his dinner.

Hiding there in the woods, reorganizing me thoughts, I decided that even though Jim was set in his twisted notions, Abner at least had what you might call flexibility. I still had a sneaking admiration for the way he could trim his sails to whatever wind that blew. Before he knew Matthew was dead, Abner had gone fishing for me with the same bait as had nearly caught me all them years ago. Except that the second time, I hadn't ... what had Michael said? ... "drooled" over

Miriam's daughter the way I had at Sophie and Imogene. If'n I'd been like Jim, still with me head stuck in a young man's dream, Abner would'a been reeling me in. When he heard Matthew was dead, he probably decided I was in league with Jim. So he softened me up with a present of nice new clothes and then sent his bully-boys to … what? Find out if Jim and me had planned it all along? Chase me off so he could have his watchers hunt the pair of us down? Maybe check whether Jonas was doing a backhanded deal with me? Perhaps just beat on me for a bit to find out what I knew? Fer certain sure he weren't still planning on fixing me up with a farm and a plump little thirteen-year-old girl.

All this ran through me mind while we was watching Jim hide the body. I thought of telling Michael that I could work me way around t'other side of the firelight and get ahead of Jim before he headed for Charton in the morning, maybe ambush him down the trail, but by the time I had the words ready to whisper, I saw she'd got her head down and were either sleeping, or making a good imitation. So I nodded off meself, waking every little now and then like I had lots of practice at from watch-keeping. Every time I took a look, Jim was still there, feeding his fire. Perhaps in his tangled mind he was keeping watch over his beloved.

Like I told yer, we was facing east. When the dawn came, it were a beauty: pearly-pink below and streaked with high clouds above. I watched the light grow downwards, first on the tree-tops, then slanting down into our side of the clearing, then crawling across the grass till I could see Jim, all hunched over, sleeping. I was doing a wriggle to get the kinks out of me back, and scratching me ribs where pine needles had found their way into me shirt, when I seen Jim's head rise.

First off, I thought he'd woken from the sun in his face, but then I seen him cant his head towards the path to The Fort, like he was listening. I nudged Michael, and when her eyes opened, I put me finger to me lips and pointed. Then there was the two of us listening in the woods, and Jim listening by the fire. As we were straining our ears until we could hear our clothes creak and our hearts thump, Jim got up, kinda shook hisself, and headed towards the bothy. Beside me, Michael twitched like she had started to stand, and then forced herself not to. She needn't have worried. Jim ignored the door and crouched down in what little shadow the low walls offered. It was like he'd disappeared.

It was then that we heard what had got him started.

Two voices, one complaining, one setting him straight. Jonas and Abner. The two of them stumbled out off the woods, Abner muddy to his knees and leaning on his stick, Jonas looking like a walking swamp from having fallen face-first into the bog. They must have started from The Fort before sundown, stopped for the night on the way, sending Fred the Watcher ahead to slog through the mud and muck in the dark to get hisself killed. Abner and Jonas had likely got going at first light, when the mosquitos had chewed them awake. As they hove into the clearing, I was still wondering what to do.

Michael twitched again, getting to hands and knees. So did I, although I had no idea what she was planning. Then I saw Jonas stop and point at where Jim hadn't hidden Fred the Watcher's corpse. 'Course they had to go see. They were bending over the body, when suddenly they both looked up. That were a bit late, considering it were a good chance that whoever had whacked Fred had to be close.

Amazingly what they'd heard weren't Jim.

The door of the bothy creaked open, and out came Sarah. At first, I couldn't figger out why she was all bent over, her hair hanging down over her face. Beside me, Michael gasped. We both scrambled to our feet.

When Sarah straightened up and took a couple steps, Michael and me saw why she was moving awkwardly: her ankles were hobbled. Her long, grey, Fort-style skirts was caked in mud to her shins, and her long sleeves up top were splattered as well. She stood and stared at Abner and Jonas, somehow looking proud and defiant, even with her hands tied, wrist crossed on wrist.

"Murderer!" Jonas yelled, even though every one of us, including him, knew that wasn't so.

Abner ignored him and took a few steps forward until he was in her face.

"Did Angel kill Jim as well?"

Abner's question told me they'd discovered Watchers One and Two. And also found someone to blame for everything: me. But no sooner I'd taken this thought aboard than everything went sideways.

Sarah went on looking at Abner eye to eye. She didn't even bother to shake her head. That took him by surprise. Abner wasn't used to being stared down, least of all by a woman. He took a step back.

Then Jackass Jonas made his big mistake. He must have thought this was his chance to assert hisself and take charge before the truth could get out, because the daft bugger stepped up, pushed Abner out of the way, took Sarah by the shoulders and shook her so's her hair rippled back and forth in the sunlight.

Michael jumped to her feet and pushed out of the trees, with me only a step behind her. Now it were daylight, I saw she were wearing breeks like a man. Wi' no skirts to trip her up, her long legs took her down slope faster than me. She let her cloak billow off her shoulders, and I nearly tripped on its swirling black cloth as I pounded down to the bothy after her.

When we was clear of the trees we both put on speed, but we weren't as quick as Jim. He came around the bothy one hand waist high, moving faster than a main boom jibing, shoved Sarah out of his way, and lit into Jonas, the morning light sliding down his long, slim knife. Then Jonas was keeling over one way, and Sarah was falling the other. Before she got to the ground Michael had her arms around her, and a good thing too, 'cause with her hands tied she were about to fall real hard.

I arrived a bit late, swung around the two women and rammed into Jim, thinking to take him down and then feed him me boots until he let go his knife. No such luck. Jim went down all right, but so did I, 'cause Abner got me in me leg with the club end of his stick. I ain't sure if he were aiming for Jim and got me instead, or the other way around. Made no difference then or now. I was down, and 'cause I know that's not a good place to be in a fight, I tried to get back up and failed when me leg gave way under me. I was part-your-hair close to a great swinging blow of Abner's stick as it went over me head and straight into Jimi's face with a wet, squidgy, crunching noise you really don't want to hear. I started to get me feet under me, and caught a glimpse of Michael, holding her right forearm in her left, standing over Sarah, who was kinda' doubled up, winded. Half a jiffy later, Abner got me in the head on the backswing, and I was out.

When I came back to meself, I was blinking at the sky, with me head pillowed on something soft. I rolled me head to starboard, and saw the shiny head of Abner's stick swinging through the air, followed by the ugly thud of someone's head being stove in. Abner was walloping on what was left of Jonas. I knew that it didn't matter to him, 'cause I'd seen him stuck by Jim's assassin's knife. The wrath of Abner were not what yer call an edifying sight, and besides it made me think I could well be next.

Me first try at getting to me feet told me that wasn't going to happen. Me face were sticky with blood, and me head hurt worse than me worst hangover ever. Trying to pick me right arm up to wipe me eyes told me I'd a broken collar bone, so I stayed right still and squinted down me nose past me right boot towards where I could see Abner's mud-splattered legs. His bloody-minded fury must have been tapering off, 'cause he was leaning on his stick, breathing hard from all the smiting he'd been doin'.

Michael must have been untying Sarah's wrists when Abner hit her. She held her left arm crooked across her chest to protect her hand and wrist. She got to her feet, stepped clear of Sarah and past what were left of Jonas and looked Abner in the eye. Abner stood there, staring back at her. Maybe he thought he were safe because she was injured and bare-handed. Maybe he was tired from all the smiting. Maybe he was curious about what she was going to say. Maybe all of that together.

Right quick, I had another shot at standing up, which weren't a success at all at all. Me left knee didn't want to work, partly 'cause it were under Jim, mainly 'cause when I moved, all I could see was a big black splodge with purple edges. The pain must have been there all along wi'out me knowing. I laid me back down, a part of me figgering that me head was pillowed on Jim's stomach, and he weren't breathing.

When the black splodge faded to a pale purple cloud I saw Sarah, bent over, trying t' get up, and Michael, 'tween her and Abner. Something were wrong with me hearing, 'cause I couldn't make out what she were saying for the roaring sound in me ears. It were like I were hearing me pain like a line of breaking waves a'tween me and what were going on.

Near as I could figger out later, Michael lit into him with all the pent-up rage of a lifetime during which she'd taken care of women who'd been bullied, and raped, and been made pregnant whether they wanted it or not, till they was used up all the way down to dying. She let go of all she'd kept in her mind since her ma died and she'd had to forget about herself and look after Sarah, and later the women and children of The Fort. She'd remembered the curses she'd left unsaid, the truth she'd swallowed rather than provoke more suffering on the people she cared for. She had forgotten none of the words she'd muffled with her pillow over years of unhappy nights and and it all came out cold and calculating.

At the time, only a few words reached me over the roaring noise in me head, but I could see them standing face to face. At first, Abner took it, probably pretending to hisself that she was only a woman and not worth arguing with. My guess is that he tried to shut her up by blithering about hope, faith, loyalty, and peace, 'cause then she really got into his face. I could see her lips shape single words, and I guessed they were names of women and children. That got to him. He took a couple steps back, trying to break out of that fierce look in her sea-green eyes, I reckon.

An' then something she said were too much for him, and his stick came up and swung at her. I must have tried to move, 'cause the purple cloud came back and the roaring got louder. Part of me wanted to let go and drown under the weight of that breaking wave of pain, but I had to know what was happening, and so I blinked away the purple in time to see the bright end of Abner's stick curve through the air. Michael jumped back, and Abner's swing went so wild the shiny head of the stick going into the ground. He staggered and nearly keeled over.

When he straightened up, Michael was back in his face again, no doubt telling him that all the loyalty he thought he had was made of fear, bullyin', pain and heart-rending suffocation of human beings what deserved better. He took it for a few heartbeats, and then something she said set him off again. He hauled his stick out of the grass and swung it at her, but quick as quick she were out of reach.

Whatever she said, it began the last Great Rage of Abner. He advanced on Michael, step by step, swinging his stick like a man cutting through tall grass. I still couldn't make out words for the roaring, but I could hear that he were shouting at her. Even through the breaking wave sounds in me head, I heard him yell every time he swung at her and she weren't there. I could see her staying beyond his reach, taunting him. He swung left to right, she danced back out of reach, right to left. Each time he swung wilder at the slim, dancing shape of her so's they zig-zagged their way up out of the clearing towards the cliff. It came to me that even as she was moving back, she was attacking, him with the truth he didn't want to hear until he didn't know or care that they had left the protection of the trees, gone out of the clearing out all the way up to the cliff-top, an' they faced each other in the wind off the sea.

When Michael got right to the lip, her back to that some-awful sheer fall to the rocks and sea below, and I saw what she was planning. Abner was getting tired, and each time he swung at her, he was slower and more awkward, so's he were near to staggering. Michael were aiming to have him take a swing that would overbalance him off the cliff-top into where she could hear the waves crash on the rocks below and then suck back to do it again, and again, and again, telling her she were in the right place to make it happen. Fer sure, it weren't telling Abner nothin'. Maybe he thought it was all going to work out jus' fine for him when with his next swing he could be rid of her and that endless story of all that he'd done wrong and never admitted to hisself, even though it must have been crawling under his skin and waking him up in the wee small hours when even the most selfish, self-centred, self-absorbed, and self-righteous man has to have second thoughts about himself. Michel danced along the grassy edge, out of reach, and he swung again so wild with fury that he staggered towards the thin lip of bare rock where nothing grew.

Sarah charged up out of the clearing towards his back. She'd finally gotten her breath, and was running to help, but where Michael were nimble and quick, Sarah's legs were all lashed up in her long, grey, mud-spattered skirts, and she moved like she were wading through deep water. Michael saw her, and Abner saw Michael see her, and in that instant Michael's plan failed. Abner hauled back his stick to swipe Michael off the cliff, but at the last moment he turned, saw Sarah, and instead of hitting Michael, Abner changed his aim for Sarah. She tripped, and instead of ramming into him, fell to her knees as' the bright end of Abner's stick swung to smash her head in.

And it would have, if Michael hadn't grabbed Abner's arm. That put the pair of them both off balance; 'cause she'd spoiled his swing. For a moment, they twirled, she light-footed, him stumbling, lurching and clumsy. Then they both was gone, down and down and down for long enough so's he'd know that she'd won, before they ended on the rocks and the sea ate the pair of them.

Over the roaring in me ears I heard me own voice screaming "No!" more times than I could count, pleading with Holy to roll back time a couple notches and let us all try it again, this time with the right ending. Holy, like aways, didn't listen. But Sarah heard, and probably just in time. She'd crawled to the edge and were looking down that eye-twisting sheer edge to where the waves smashed and sucked back and smashed again. I think she might'a gone after them, and over the years that thought has told me that I ain't entirely useless.

Sarah backed away from that eye-dragging view down the cliff, and made her sad way back to see who had been screaming. She saw I was alive, propped me up so's I weren't leaning on Jim's corpse, covered me with Michael's cloak, and walked all the way back to The

Fort — not that I knew, 'cause I was clean out of me somewhat dented head.

Anyway, she came back with Miriam and a couple more women, one of the older boys what could be trusted, and most important, a big, strong horse. They strapped me alongside the horse, Sarah gave me something for the pain, and off we went, me in me own little world, right off me chump

Nineteen

Well, that's it.

I have to thank you for sneaking out yesterday wi'out what the books call "further ado." You needed to know, but it were a savage moment for all of us, then and now.

What's that?

Yeah, you're right. It ain't over. It never is. Even when I woke up to find I was lying alongside a couple of dead men and was wondering when I'd be the next one to croak, I still knew I'd be all right. And I was.

It were days in sick-bay at The Fort before there was anything I remember except short stabs of pain and long stretches of nothing but wicked strange dreams thanks to what Sarah gave me to stop me moaning and groaning. It were weeks before I could stand, and months before I could stagger around the sick bay in the big white house what they'd decided to call The Home. Soon as I could think without me head throbbing, I tried to say thankee to Sarah and the women what was looking after me, but they weren't having none of it — in a nice way, that is.

After I'd started making sense, I went over and over in me mind how Michael had almost danced Abner over the cliff, and I felt again the sick emptiness of seeing she was gone. One night, when I was blubbering about the all-consuming unfairness that I was alive and Michael weren't, Sarah came in, looked me over, and said: "Talk."

I started muttering and cursing and whinging long enough that she sat down beside me bed. Dunno what I said, but there was a lot of sniffing and considerable blubbering, and not just by me. Later, when we was both beginning to talk reasonable, Sarah told me what Michael said to trigger Abner's final blind rage.

Back there on the cliff-edge, Michael had told Abner he'd not fathered any of the children he thought were his. Now you got to know that Abner was hearing all this from Michael, The Fort's healer and the collector of everyone's secrets. That must have been bad enough for him, but then she went on to say that all the women he'd ever gotten into knew it as well.

None of them had said anything for fear of Abner's watchers. They'd all known that when he'd lost interest, or spotted another woman that he fancied, Abner turned the last one over to Jonas and the watchers, no doubt thinking, hoping and who knows, perhaps even praying that when the babies arrived they were his. It started with the women who first landed at The Fort, then the sister-wives, later still, the younger-every-year girls. And Michael had told him that everybody knew.

He were still denying it as they went over the edge.

But enough of that. I still got stuff to tell the two of you.

Somewhen during the process of getting meself back together, I gimped me way into a meeting of everybody, sat with me gammy leg on a stool, and wondered what they was going t 'do with me. As the women trooped into the big meeting-room I noticed that except for three farmers, there weren't any men. Not many older boys, neither. It seemed that the few men left had been told to move out for the good of their health, as in "leave while you're still living." I didn't ask what happened to them that didn't walk away, and when I asked about the two watchers I'd left alive but uncomfortable, nobody knew nothing.

All of which made me ask meself if I was next. I wondered how I'd go anywhere — did I tell you me boat got burned? The idiot boatbuilder let his pitch-pot fire get out of hand, and by the time he woke up to it, she'd burned to the waterline. He had the decency to send a boy with the news, and me money up front, but on top of everything else, it were a misery. I'd had more'n twenty years aboard that ketch. I knew her and her ways.

Speaking of burnin', that's what they did with the bodies at the clearing. Dragged them into the bothy, threw in a whole lot of wood, and set fire to it. Nothing anybody could do about Abner and Michael, though. The sea had them, and didn't give them back.

What happened at the meeting, you ask.

Well, I'll tell yer. Y'needed to know the background to understand what was going through me mind as the folks assembled. Looking at me foot on the stool in front of me told me how blamed useless I were. All I could do was listen.

Anyway, after a whole lot of shuffling about, and once a few women had and talked a bit about how bad it had been, and a few more about how good it could be if only they could get organized, they all looked at Sarah, and she took charge of the meeting. So then they got to planning. You have no idea how long that took. I nearly shouted, "Stop blathering you silly women. Jus' put Sarah in charge, and do like she says," but I didn't, and it was a good thing, too, because a whole lot of talking later, Sarah WAS in charge, but it wasn't like she took over. Gradually, it came to me that she had been nudging things along, never ordering, never commanding, always listening even to the drivelling nonsense some of them spouted, talking sweet reason until it somehow worked out sensible, and everyone got ready to go away feeling that they'd all decided together.

Everyone but me, sitting there looking foolish with me leg on a stool. No boat. No crew. Couldn't walk. Couldn't ride. No knowledge of farming. Nothing to offer out of a life devoted to the art of staying alive. An' that was what I was thinking even before some o' them started talking about me being the one what brought Jim back to trigger all the carnage what followed.

That was where I was when Sarah stood up and told them I was the man what had brought them aboard *Tidewalker*, looked after them on the voyage north, and had near died trying to protect Michael. An' then they all looked at each other and whispered. Some nodded. A few shook their heads, which weren't encouraging.

They let me stay. More'n that, they took right good care of me, until I could look after meself, re-build this old house, and share in the life of what we all decided to call Matris — a word meaning mother in some old language.

Y' know, by and large, Matris worked. Years went by. Boys and girls grew to be men and women. Matris was raided by that pirate Mufrid who got wind of where we were, and kidnapped a bunch of our best boys. Some young women left, some came back. More'n a few women sat in them chairs where you are right now, and chased away their guilt and shame by sharing their secrets with me — secrets what I ain't going to share with you nor nobody else.

I'm rambling again, but don't yer go yet. There's still things I have to tell the two of you, starting with you, lad.

You both know better than most about The Wandering, what that man Zubin started right after the City of the Sea, when he'd dropped me and me fellow misfits into that ketch. From that day on, so they say, those big schooners stayed at sea, year after year, until more than a hundred years had passed. Well, that last part ain't true, 'cause I'm still alive and kicking, but there's no doubt those schooners were launched a long time ago, when men knew how to shape them big hulls and rig ships like we can't do now.

What folks don't know or can't do, they make stories about, y' know? Like ships that sail forever. People take a bit of truth, and a fact or two, and like an old woman knitting with whatever wool she can find in her basket, they weave in a little hope, a fair deal of fear, the occasional mystery, and like as not a prophecy, too, — just like in all them tales old Holy got his amanuensises to write for him.

You know that, don't you, lad, 'cause you was the one foretold what brought The Wandering to an end. Now, don't shake yer head. Yer part of the legend, and whether you believe it or not, you got a destiny, and you with him, lass.

What's that?

No, lass, I ain't yer grandfather, though I'd be proud if t'were so. There ain't nothing between me and Sarah except for me everlasting respect for how she midwifed Matris out of The Fort, and gave a crew of badly used women and children good lives and the self-respect that comes of knowing they did it themselves. I've been telling you about men what looked good but did unholy wrong to them that they commanded, led, guided, whatever. Sarah, your grandmother, she's different. She helps everyone discover what's best for every last one of us. She don't know how good she is, 'cause she keeps telling herself she ain't up there with Michael.

Michael. I dunno how Sarah remembers her big sister, but when I say the name, I still can see those wide blue eyes on the skinny girl who was looking after her sister, no matter what it cost her.

What's that? I sorta drifted off for a bit, there. Who was yer grand-dad?

Well, lass, you know full well, that Matris don't keep no ledger like old Holy's book of Leviticus, filled with lists of who did the begetting and who got begot. That ain't something we talk about here, 'cause to do so would be to stir up shame where there shouldn't be none for neither the women concerned nor their daughters and sons. So go figger dates and times for yerself, remembering that nobody can be certain sure, except for those what know and don't want to talk about it.

Remember that bad things are done by good men and good can come from men who look like they're all bad.

An' that's that. I'm powerful dry from sharing me story with you two, and now it's done, you don't have to listen to an old man rattling on…

Well, since yer offering, I don't mind if I do.

Thank'ee for that.

An' here's to you, too.

Fin

A Personal Note From the Author

I wanted to write from age eight, if not before, because I wanted to live in the worlds of the books I loved. Somehow education taught me that writers were different, superior, gifted, inspired and much, much smarter than me. So I studied literature, and eventually taught it. I nibbled at writing stories from time to time, but only completed a book that was published in 2011, three years after I retired. Now I'm pushing 80, with five books published, the first by a small house, the rest self-published, for which I make no apology -- I don't have time left to start as if I was in my 20s, and work my way into recognition through magazines, collections, and so on up to a so-called "serious" publisher. What I'm doing now is writing because I love it. From writing I learn about life, about me, about boats and sailing, about books, about love, about people around me and about looking forward. What I do is definitely not an economic endeavour. After I'd taken the decision to go on writing, it became all the better for not being about success measured in dollars and cents.

Notwithstanding all this, I don't recommend or advise anything that I've done with the exception of one golden principle: **write your own book**. The moment I stopped trying to write **in imitation of** this or that style, or genre, or him, or her, I started to write in my own voice, and it all became worth while.

If you enjoyed this story, please let me know.
email: colophon@storm.ca

Also by Seymour Hamilton

The Astreya Trilogy (Fireship / Cortero Press, 2011)

Book I: *The Voyage South*

Book II: *The Men of the Sea*

Book III: *The Wanderer's Curse*

River of Stones (Colophon / Old Salt Press 2020)

Available through Amazon.

Angel's Share

Available through Amazon or as pdf, mobi, epub

available from SeymourHamilton.com

The foregoing three stories are all in the same imaginative universe

The Laughing Princess (Açedrex, 2014),

Illustrated by Shirley MacKenzie

Another universe which includes dragons

The Hippies Who Meant It (Colophon / Scribl 2015)

Set on the North Mountain of Nova Scotia and involving those who homesteaded there in the 70s

All but *Angel's Share* are available in ebook, paperback and soon in audio read by Seymour Hamilton, through Amazon and Scribl.

Author's Website: SeymourHamilton.com

If you enjoy books with Nautical Settings

...there's more from Old Salt Press

Hellfire Corner by Alaric Bond

Alaric Bond's latest nautical adventure departs the Age of Fighting Sail where his other 13 novels are set, and instead goes aboard Motor Torpedo Boats and Motor Gun Boats of the Coastal Forces in the English Channel during WWII.

Water Ghosts by Linda Collison

"I see things other people don't see; I hear things other people don't hear." Fifteen-year-old James McCafferty is an unwilling sailor aboard a traditional Chinese Junk operated as adventure-therapy for troubled teens. Once at sea, James believes the ship is being taken over by the spirits of courtiers who fled the Imperial palace during the Ming Dynasty, more than 600 years earlier, and sailing to its doom.

Perilous Shore by Chris Durbin

The sixth Carlisle and Holbrook naval adventure. It is the latest of a series of books that follows Carlisle and Holbrooke through the Seven Years War and into the 1760s when relations between Britain and her restless American Colonies are tested to breaking point. Look out for the seventh in the Carlisle Holbrooke series, coming soon.

The Discovery of Tahiti by Joan Druett

Romance and the islands have gone hand-in-hand since the bare-breasted young women of Tahiti gave a rousing welcome to the 18th century European adventurers who discovered the island. But it was not just a tropical port of call that Captain Wallis and his men found, for their tales of golden girls and a majestic island queen became a foundation stone of the Romantic Movement, an enduring inspiration for writers, artists, filmmakers ... and mutineers."

Evening Gray Morning Red by Rick Spillman.

A young American sailor must escape his past and the clutches of the Royal Navy, in the turbulent years just before the American Revolutionary War. In the spring of 1768, Thom Larkin, a 17-year-old sailor, is caught by a Royal Navy press gang. He runs afoul of the cruel and corrupt Lieutenant Dudingston. Years later, after escaping, Thom again crosses paths with his old foe in Narragansett Bay. Thom Larkin must face the guns of the Royal Navy, with only his wits, an unarmed packet boat, and a sandbar.

Blackwell's Paradise by VE Ulett

The repercussions of a court martial and the ill will of powerful men at the Admiralty pursue Royal Navy captain James Blackwell into the Pacific. Even if Captain Blackwell and Mercedes survive the venture into the world of early 19th-century exploration, can they emerge unchanged, with their love intact? The mission to the Great South Sea will test their loyalties and strength and define the characters of Captain Blackwell and his lady in Blackwell's Paradise.

Britannia's Innocent by Antoine Vanner

This is the eighth volume of the Dawlish Chronicles historical naval fiction series. A prequel to the existing seven "Britannia's...." novels, the action take place in 1864, when the young Nicholas Dawlish is still an innocent. He finds himself plunged into the horrors of a siege, involving shore-bombardment, raiding and battle in the cold North Sea. He will need to learn fast.

A Sneak Peek at The Astreya Trilogy

The following is an excerpt from *The Astreya Trilogy, Book I, The Voyage South.* All three books of the trilogy are available in paperback or electronic format.

The Astreya Trilogy

Chapter 1:

In which Astreya fights with Yan, and Alana passes on a gift

The young men of the Village pushed and shoved Astreya along the shoreline between outcroppings of rock at the sea's edge, and then into a little bay below the cliffs, where he could not escape. When they had formed a circle around him, Yan, the chief tormentor, shouldered his way into the wild-eyed ring. He was a heavy-set, powerful-looking boy with shoulders that began just below his earlobes. Solid muscles strained his shirt-sleeves, and his thick forearms ended in stubby-fingered hands. His reddish hair grew almost down to his eyebrows, his youthful beard was patchy, and he breathed with his mouth half open, revealing wide-spaced teeth. Astreya was as slim as Yan was bulky, dark as he was fair. He stood almost casually, but behind the pose, he was tight as coiled spring.

Yan lumbered forward; Astreya dodged, caught a big upraised arm, pivoted, pulled and stepped back. Yan fell face-forward, and the ring of youths distorted into an oval. Yan scrambled to his feet, spitting sand.

"Fight like a man!" Yan shouted.

"Sure," replied Astreya. "If you can find me one. You're nothing but a boy."

He stuck out his chin and stroked his hand over his short, black beard, mocking Yan's pale tufts of facial hair. Yan growled wordlessly. Someone shoved at Astreya's back, but instead of falling, Astreya dived, rolled on his shoulder and came up face-to-face with Yan, so close that neither could hit the other.

"Where d'ya learn to do that?"

"Scarm."

"What kind of wrestlin' do you learn from a one-armed man? Hey, little blackhead goody-goody? Spend a lot of time with Scarm do ya? Readin' stuff? An' what else do you do?"

"He's twice the man you are, with spare parts left over."

"Oh, he is, is he? So and how do you know? And what's he been teaching you about? Before stuff, that nobody cares codswallop to know? Tell me, blackhead, what are you readin' about now?"

"Triangles," said Astreya. "Square-corner triangles, and how their sides always work out to be three, four and five."

Yan paused just an instant too long before forcing a laugh.

"Some good that'll do ya. Tryin' to make yourself special. Well, blackhead, you are special. Special strange. Son of a … a … stranger. Spendin' time with that crazy old one-armed man Scarm who's lost his grip." Yan paused. "One-armed man who's lost his grip. Hey, that's good, ain't it?

Some of the boys laughed, whether they got the point or not.

"Very good, Yan. Very funny. A joke. And you got a laugh. Beginner's luck."

Yan fell back a step, half-crouched, and readied himself to grab for the first hold.

"Yan," said Astreya, "This is stupid. Let's all go home."

"Are you calling me stupid?"

Astreya shrugged. Yan lunged forward to grab him in a bear hug, but Astreya dropped, crouched, and kicked at the back of Yan's knee, felling the big red-haired lad to the sand. Red-faced under his ginger hair, he scrambled to his feet again and aimed a roundhouse swing at Astreya's head. Astreya ducked and circled to his left, glancing over his shoulder for a weak spot in the ring of clasped hands.

"You – you stranger. You got no business speaking to my girl."

"That's her business, not yours."

"She's mine. And you're not going to steal her."

"I wouldn't want to."

Rob, a slope-shouldered, long-armed boy just coming into his man's strength, grabbed Astreya from behind, pinning his arms.

"Yan, you goin' t'let this black-haired stranger mess with our girls?"

Yan glared at Astreya from under his thatch of unruly hair. Astreya slid down out of the hold, but two other young men snatched at his arms and hauled them in opposite directions. Astreya tried to brace on one and kick the other, but before he could do so, Yan charged head-down into his unprotected middle, doubling him over. Astreya fell face down into the sand, gasping for breath, taking his two captors with him. Two more joined in to help, and a milling, grunting, sweat-and-sand-streaked pile held Astreya, spread-eagled on the black sand beach.

"Turn him over!"

They tried to follow Yan's order, but Astreya kicked and struggled, knocking two back on their heels. But the two who held his arms did not let go. Astreya spat sand, some of which reached Yan's face, redoubling his fury. However, the pack's enthusiasm was waning. All but Yan found the victory unsatisfactory, since it had been at the price of breaking the Village's code of one-on-one wrestling. Fights among both boys and men ended when one person was pinned. There was no wounding or killing, because there never had been.

"That's enough, eh?" said Cam, the smallest of the group, who had been pushed aside early in the struggle. His mouse-blonde hair stuck to a cut over one eye, and his oversized jacket was torn, even though he had not come close to Astreya in the confusion of hands and feet.

No one heeded, although Yan felt his followers' eyes on him. He shook his head, sweat flipping off the ends of his hair. His mind slipped to the work of killing fish, chickens, rabbits and sheep -- the business necessary to eating and living in the world they all shared. He picked up a stone and advanced on Astreya, a matter-of-fact purpose in his eyes.

"Hold it," he said.

Indecision froze the minds of Astreya's captors as they saw the upraised stone, and they loosened their grip. Astreya squirmed convulsively, broke free, scrambled to his feet, stumbled backward and stood with his shoulders against the cliff that loomed above the tiny beach.

Yan advanced on Astreya like a sleepwalker, shrugging off Cam, who was too small and light to restrain him. His big, work-hardened fist came up. For an instant, all of Astreya's swiftness and agility ebbed out of him.

"Duck!" Cam screamed, breaking the spell.

Astreya saw Yan's hand tighten on the jagged stone, saw its sharp edges, saw the clumsy weapon coming at him, saw the ring of aghast faces, saw the encroaching sea behind them, saw the stone again, and knew he had ample time to side-step before the stone smacked on the cliff close to his ear, crumbling in Yan's hand. The sound snapped the murderous sequence of events, leaving all them at a loss. Six attackers faced Astreya, unsure what to do next. Yan sucked split finger-ends. Astreya scanned past faces as expressionless as if they had all been fresh-woken from sleep.

"Take a look behind you," said Astreya calmly.

The incoming sea had more than halved the beach. Waves foamed over black, jagged rock on either side of the little bay. Their footprints had vanished, and the marks of the scuffle were being eaten away by successive waves. They stared at the water in a horrified fascination, realised their peril, and shrank back beside Astreya, their backs joining his against the cliff.

"We can still make it back around the point," said Yan.

"In a goat's arse," said Astreya. "You'll be dragged out to sea with the first wave."

"We're going to be in deep, and soon," said Cam.

"We'll have to climb out," said Astreya.

The sea hissed on the sand as each wave pulled back from an ever-higher watermark. The undertow rattled pebbles where they had walked dry-shod.

Astreya alone was not hypnotised by the steadily-approaching sea. While the others stared blankly, he turned towards the cliff.

"This way," he said, looking up at a crack in the black cliff. Above their heads, the crack opened to a fissure and then to a chimney that led up to where the roots of a pine tree knuckled over the cliff-edge, far above them, but the rock where he touched was slicked with green slime, and his fingers could not find a hold.

"You can't get up that," said Cam. "Nobody can. We're done for."

"No we're not," said Astreya. "Take off your belts and buckle them together," said Astreya. "Then lift me up. I'm tallest and lightest."

"He'll just get up there and leave us," said Yan.

"Don't be stupid," said Astreya. "It's the only way."

"Don't call me stupid!" Yan shouted.

"Well, don't say stupid things," said Astreya.

Something in his voice cut through their fear and indecision, and they did as they were told, even though under different circumstances, they might have sided with Yan, ignored Astreya, or told him in a few crude words not to think himself better than they.

"Right," said Astreya, as the sea herded them closer. "We need three to stand here against the rock and bend over. Cam, you're light, you can climb on their backs. Now if everyone brace against the cliff..."

"Rob and Yan, you're strongest," said Cam, who had seen what was to be done. "You be the bottom row." He clutched at the waistband of his breeks as they threatened to slip off his hips now that his belt was gone.

Yan braced his hands on the cliff, his head down, his mind confused by the succession of sudden changes. Blood dripped from his fingers onto the sand at his feet. Rob put his shoulder to Yan's hip, and Cam struggled up Rob's back onto Yan's shoulders. Then Astreya clambered up the clumsy human ladder. Cam's canvas jacket ripped as Astreya got first one knee and then the other onto his shoulders. Steadying himself against the cliff, he stood and reached beyond the sea-slick rock to the first possible handholds of strong, dry stone. At that moment, the improvised stack of bodies disintegrated, and all but Astreya tumbled in a heap onto the sand below. For a moment, he dangled from his hands. He scrabbled with his feet and pulled mightily. First his forearm, then his chest and finally a knee made it to the first ledge in the widening cleft. He clung panting to the rock, felt his heartbeat pound in his throat, and momentarily was unable to move. Then as his breathing steadied, he recovered his calm. He looked up at the rocky scramble to the cliff-top, and Yan's words came back to him. It would be easy to continue on up the cliff, leaving the others behind. He hesitated only for an instant, and then bracing his shoulders on one side of the crack, he planted his feet on the other, and unwound the rope of belts from his waist. He lowered one end down to the upturned faces below.

"Yan first, then Rob," he shouted, taking a turn of the belts around a spur of rock.

They all saw what had to be done.

"Good idea, 'Streya," said Cam. "We can do it."

Yan took hold of the dangling belts and scrambled hand over hand up the slick rock to the foot and handholds that began where Astreya braced himself. Avoiding Astreya's eyes as he clambered over him, Yan climbed on up the widening gully. Sand and small stones rattled down on Astreya, bouncing off his shoulders and stinging the back of his neck.

One after the other, the rest half climbed, half hauled themselves up the cliff-face. Without the improvised rope, they would not have been able to scale the water-polished, seaweed-slick stone, and every one of them knew it. They stared up at Astreya, climbed towards him, looked into his grey-green eyes, took his hand and accepted his help into the chimney of dry, firm rock, where climbing was easy.

Eventually they all stood at the cliff-top, looking down on Astreya's head and shoulders as he scrambled up towards them. With sidelong glances at each other, and no words said, they collected their belts and set off for their homes. Cam was last to leave. He stood, fitting his belt back into his oversized breeks, looking quizzically at Astreya with his head on one side.

"'Streya, how did you do that?"

"What?"

"Why ain't you dead with a rock in your head?"

"I … ah … just was quicker than he was, I guess."

"Quicker? One moment you was a goner. Next moment, you're an arm's length away, Yan hit the cliff, and you were tellin' us what to do, like you were explainin' that the sun comes up in the morning."

Astreya could not explain, even to himself, how time had slowed for him, bringing with it complete confidence.

" Yan ain't goin' to say it, fer sure," said Cam with a grin, "so thanks for saving our lives."

Before Astreya could reply, Cam turned and walked away, his shapeless, torn jacket pulled around him. Astreya took a step back to the cliff edge, knelt, and looked past the grass they had crushed at its lip, down the steep gully to the water-darkened rock where the sea heaved and fell. Down there on the beach that was now under water, he had experienced something he had never felt before, and did not fully comprehend. He was proud that his strategy had worked, that he had organised and led young men who moments before had been ready to see him humiliated. But there was something more: for a moment, he could have left them all to drown. The realisation made him giddy, as if at the last moment he had pulled back from stepping off the cliff top. Slowly, Astreya turned and headed towards his home.

As the last light faded above the rocky western ridge high above the Village, Astreya opened the door of his home. When Alana raised her head and turned swiftly towards the door, her white hair, loose for the night, flared in a candle-lit blur. Her quick glance took in his ripped and dirt-caked clothes, and then the cut knuckles on the hand with which he tried to hide a bruised cheek. Silently, she pointed to a chair beside the table, and bent to scoop a bowl full of warm water from the iron pot above the fire. Astreya tried not to wince as she sponged dirt and dried blood from his face, forearms and hands. To avoid her eyes, he watched her shadow on the whitewashed walls. Eventually, when she had finished tending his cuts, he answered the question her silence had been asking.

"It was all because I drew a picture of Tina, and Yan saw it."

"Was it a good picture?"

"Well, you could see it was her. I caught the way she looks a little to one side, so she seems to be sweet on you, but it's really because she doesn't hear that well."

"I didn't know that."

"You have to watch closely, just like she does to see people's lips."

"And you've been watching her?

"Only to draw her."

"Which you did today."

"Yeah. Down where they're preparing the boats for the season. She was sitting on the wharf, and I had my drawing stuff with me, and, well, it seemed like a good idea at the time. But Yan came up behind me and saw."

"And then?"

"He said it was stealing, and that she was his. And then I said something I shouldn't have."

"Yes?"

"I told him he was an idiot who didn't own anybody, least of all Tina."

"He was angry."

"Oh yes. He wouldn't take a run at me, because, well, I've stymied him before, and he didn't want to take the chance in front of her."

"And Tina?"

"She's the same as the rest of the girls. She knows that a man should be fair-haired, big-jawed and blue-eyed. I'm the green-eyed blackhead with the dark curly beard. I'm a stranger."

When Astreya almost spat the words he hated, Alana spoke to move the story forward.

"So what did Yan do?"

"He got a few of the other fellows together. They followed me. I thought I'd lost them by going around the headland at low tide. My mistake. They caught me."

"And then?"

"We tussled a bit, and then we all got caught by the tide, and we had to climb up the cliff."

There was a long pause, as both of them contemplated what Astreya had not said.

"Stupid pictures. I never should have started. Now everybody knows I draw things."

"Secrets have a habit of getting out."

"Like Scarm teaching me to wrestle."

"You should call him Ian."

"Everyone calls him Scarm. He doesn't mind."

"He's been good to you. You should show him respect."

"Mother, I do. The last time I came home like this, it was a long time ago, and I was a lot younger. You remember, because you cleaned me up, just the way you're doing now. Next day, Scarm took me aside and showed me a few moves."

"Did you thank him?"

"Of course. And for the other stuff he taught me."

"The other stuff?"

"You know, the ciphering, the triangles, the puzzles, the stories. He said my … my father … would have wanted me to learn."

"So he would. Does anyone know he was teaching you?"

"I don't think so, leastways, not exactly. They know I've been into his books, but most of them can't read anything beyond a list of fish or their own names, so that they don't know and don't care. Besides, Scarm keeps all but a few of his books secret, so that nobody will know how many he has."

Alana looked into her son's eyes, and saw that there was no point in pressuring him further about the fight, or anything else he might have kept from her.

"Secrets," said Alana slowly. "I've kept too many from you."

"You've what? I thought I was the one who was keeping secrets …"

"You don't know enough about your father," she began.

She looked into Astreya's eyes for signs of rejection. Astreya stared back at her, noticing once again the contrast between her youthful face and the white hair that framed it.

"There's so much you don't know, Astreya, because I don't know, either. Or I'm not sure. I've never lied, but I have been keeping things from you. It's because I feared for you, what with people so unwilling to see what a good man he was. But it was wrong of me to hide your father from you -- his strangeness, I mean."

The word hung between them, echoing the many times they had both heard it in the Village as an accusation and rebuke. This was why she had kept him to herself as much as possible when he was a baby and then a little boy, why she had tried to find ways of dissuading him from going to sea; and this was also why as he matured, they had slowly grown apart. They were both aware that over the most recent year or two, they had laughed together less often, and while they remained polite and even distantly affectionate, they were separated by Astreya's increasing need to become a man. Though they had not spoken of it, they both knew that a boy came of age in the Village when a skipper chose him as crew. The Villagers of his own age saw him as a stranger, he had responded by isolating himself, and this lessened his chances of being chosen, but he felt the need to go to sea, even though he knew that Alana dreaded the moment when he would sail onto the ocean that had taken his father's life. He was willing to be different, indeed, he took a perverse pleasure in it, but when Alana used the word "strange" of his father, a sudden anger hardened his voice.

"Strange, Mother? Foreign? Different? How strange? I don't think of my father as strange. Scarm doesn't think he was strange. Scarm always tries to get my – his – our – name right. If it wasn't for him – and you too, Mother – I wouldn't be able to read. I wouldn't have learned stuff people knew Before or …" he stopped as he saw the expression on her face, understanding for the first time that even to his mother Alana, he, too, was strange.

They stared at each other as if a cold wind had suddenly blown them apart. Alana deliberately stood up, went into her room and returned with the leather-bound box that her husband had made. She put her hand on its domed top, and turned towards her son.

"I gave you some of what is in here, when you were younger. You've seen the pictures he made. I think maybe you started drawing because of them. Now...."

She undid the clasp, threw the box open and stood aside, her head erect and her voice firm.

"You must follow your own way, my son," she said. "I cannot walk it for you. Forgive me if I have ever tried to hold your father's memory from you more than I should have, but ... but I was not sure what to tell you. Some of what he said was beyond me. Some things didn't make sense. I couldn't explain them to you, because I didn't understand it myself."

Astreya took a pace towards the box, and then looked down at his mother, very conscious that he overtopped her height by more than a hand span. She drew Astreya to her for brief hug, and then deliberately released him. Blinking away tears, she busied herself with banking up the fire for the night. When she stood to go to her room, he was kneeling in front of the box, turning through bundles of bark and paper tied together with strands of wool that had not been undone in his lifetime. Silently, Alana moved out of the candlelight and went to her room, leaving Astreya alone in the candle-light, poring over the clues to his father's life. She lay wide-awake in her bed, knowing that her son would leave the Village to solve the mystery he had inherited, and wondering whether she had set him on a path to destruction.

That night, Astreya slept little, and so also the next. He already knew the plain words his father had written to help Alana learn to read and write, and which she had in turn used to encourage him when he first began his schooling. But what he read now was different, disordered and confusing. He had hoped to learn more about his father, but he was baffled by enigmatic references to a seafaring life unlike anything the Village could offer. There were pages of perplexing drawings marked only with symbols and numbers, interspersed with diagrams, some of them composed of interlocked triangles. They were bewilderingly unlike the triangles Scarm had shown him how to solve, first as mental exercise, then as a way of drawing charts. And then there were sketches of tall-sailed boats with many masts, the like of which Astreya had never seen or imagined. And then there were columns of figures interspersed with letters. And more symbols. And always the sea was behind it all.

At the bottom of the chest, Astreya found a little leather bag, and a small notebook. He emptied the bag onto the table, revealing about a dozen greenish pebbles, each about the size of the last joint of his little finger, and two larger stones, about the size and shape of an onion. He frowned as he examined them carefully, because he could see nothing that distinguished them from any handful of river stones. After a few moments, he put them back in the bag and dropped it into the chest.

The notebook was more promising. It had been made to be carried in a pocket, and it appeared to distill the cryptic notes that made up most of the writing in the trunk. Most of the pages were empty, many held sketches of boats, some of them with details of standing and running rigging unlike anything used by the Village fleet. Several pages reminded Astreya of the glimpses he had seen of Scarm's Born and Buried book, because they appeared to use the same shorthand or code, interspersed occasionally with the name of some important member of a Village family. He recognised one page as a map of the Village, the fjord and its seaward approaches. The last page held words that Astreya first thought might be part of a song.

> hand of gian far draws on shore
>
> star sets in song where stones roll in the tide
>
> son of or on plots a course to the city of the sea
>
> as dim clasps light no more

The words were written in letters that had been gone over and over, as if the writer had wanted to carve them into the page. What his father had meant was not clear at all. Unlike the rest of the book, where words were complete though often obscure, this cryptic message was confused and apparently misspelled. He wondered if the third word lacked a t, making the word into 'giant' – but that made little more sense. The words were legible, but seemingly pointless. A star setting in the sea was possible, but in a song? Son of whom? Had he meant to write 'off'? What was meant by or on? In which case, how could someone be a son 'off or on'? Had his father meant to write 'one' rather than 'on?' Had he just been a careless speller? Where and what was the city of the sea? Were there words missing in the last line? What was a dim, and how could it clasp light? The meaning of the riddle – if that was what it was – eluded him. He showed the verse to Alana, but she only shook her head.

The book fascinated Astreya, no page more than this one. Night by night, he pored over the legacy of words and drawings, and as he did so, Astreya grew subtly older and more distant in Alana's eyes. Although the moment of his parting from her hung ever heavier over both of them, neither could speak of it.

While the spring moon filled, they lived in growing discomfort. Each day, Astreya was part of the Village's preparations for the fishing season, and each night he sat silent, sometimes thinking, sometimes reading what his father had written, while she attended to her stitching, more often than not with the needle idle in her hands. A beeswax candle beside her, its delicate perfume unnoticed, she watched shadows flicker across her son's face, and saw in him an echo of the man she had married but never fully understood.

www.ingramcontent.com/pod-product-compliance
Lightning Source LLC
Chambersburg PA
CBHW070309120726
47910CB00007B/2405